MURDER AT THE HOTEL

CARMEL COVE MYSTERY SERIES

M A COMLEY

JEAMEL PUBLISHING LIMITED

New York Times and USA Today bestselling author M A Comley
Published by Jeamel Publishing limited
Copyright © 2019 M A Comley
Digital Edition, License Notes

This is a work of fiction. Names, characters, places and incidents are a product of the author's imagination or are used fictitiously, and any resemblance to actual persons living or dead, business establishments, events or locales is entirely coincidental.

OTHER BOOKS BY THE AUTHOR

Criminal Actions (Hero Series #5) Coming January 2020
Sole Intention (Intention series #1)
Grave Intention (Intention series #2)
Devious Intention (Intention #3)
Merry Widow (A Lorne Simpkins short story)
It's A Dog's Life (A Lorne Simpkins short story)
A Time To Heal (A Sweet Romance)
A Time For Change (A Sweet Romance)
High Spirits
The Temptation series (Romantic Suspense/New Adult Novellas)
Past Temptation
Lost Temptation
Cozy Mystery Series
Murder at the Wedding
Murder at the Hotel
Murder by the Sea (Coming December 2019)
Tempting Christa (A billionaire romantic suspense co-authored by Tracie Delaney #1)
Avenging Christa (A billionaire romantic suspense co-authored by Tracie Delaney #2)

ACKNOWLEDGMENTS

Thank you as always to my rock, Jean, I'd be lost without you in my life.

Special thanks as always go to @studioenp for their superb cover design expertise.

My heartfelt thanks go to my wonderful editor Emmy Ellis, my proofreaders Joseph, Barbara and Jacqueline for spotting all the lingering nits.

KEEP IN TOUCH WITH THE AUTHOR

Twitter
https://twitter.com/Melcom1

Blog
http://melcomley.blogspot.com

Facebook
http://smarturl.it/sps7jh

Newsletter
http://smarturl.it/8jtcvv

BookBub
www.bookbub.com/authors/m-a-comley

MURDER AT THE HOTEL

M. A. Comley

1

---

*R*uth Morgan curled up with James on the couch in their quaint cottage, more out of necessity than desire, both of them togged up in their winter coats, woollen bobble hats and gloves.

"I wish the damn heating engineer would hurry up. What time did he say he was coming today? It's freezing in here," Ruth asked in between her teeth chattering.

"Two o'clock, give or take an hour or so." James' reply was muffled against the scarf he had wrapped around his face.

"I can't stand it much longer. Are you sure it wouldn't be warmer if we went out?"

James laughed. "Hardly, it's minus eight out there."

Ruth reached over and patted her Golden Labrador, Ben, on the head. He was scrunched up beside her, covered in a blanket, also shivering. "What a day for the boiler to break down."

"I think it's been on the blink for weeks. I should have paid more attention to it, so yes, it's my fault."

Ruth angled her head to kiss him on the cheek. "We've both been super busy, what with trying to get Carolyn, Keith and the boys settled into their new home for Christmas. You've also been snowed under at work as well. Please don't feel guilty, these things happen. I bet boilers break down all the time in the dead of winter."

James chuckled. "Did you have to mention the *dead* word? Because at the moment I feel on the brink." He shuddered beside her.

"Can you imagine what those poor men must go through, the ones who choose to explore the coldest places on Earth? You've got to ask why, haven't you? They must be out of their minds, right?"

"Each to their own as my old gran used to say. If we were all the same, the world would be a pretty dull place to live."

"I suppose so. Gosh, I'm too cold to even venture into the kitchen to make a cup of coffee. Do you fancy doing it? I'll love you forever if you do." She smiled and fluttered her eyelashes, surprised they hadn't turned brittle and snapped off in the freezing temperatures.

"You only say that when you want something." James got to his feet and stared down at her.

She pouted. "That's so not true. You know I love you to the moon and back and twice around the other planets in our solar system."

"And yet you refuse to bite the bullet and marry me."

Ruth inwardly sighed. *Why is it that every subject under the universe we discuss lately comes back to the same topic? I decided long ago that I'm a commitment-phobe. Sometimes it eats away at me so much, I hate myself. How James puts up with me, I'll never know.* Nevertheless, she loved him. "I will, eventually," she promised for the umpteenth time in the past few months alone.

If James had been any other man she'd gone out with, she would have dumped him for his persistence long ago. Didn't that prove something?

His shoulders slumped, and he left the room. In the kitchen, she heard the cups and the fridge door taking the brunt of his foul mood.

She hugged Ben. He moaned as usual, the same way he always did when she showed him an ounce of affection. "You still love me, don't you, boy?"

He licked the side of her face. She smiled.

"I'd be lost without you by my side, keeping my life balanced and heading in the right direction," she whispered.

The phone rang. She eased Ben aside and reached across the arm of the couch to answer it. "Hello?"

"Hello, love, how are you coping with no heat?" her mother's voice rippled down the line.

"Hi, Mum. We're coping, just about. The engineer is due anytime soon. How are you doing?"

Since her mother and father had retired and bought a luxury campervan, they spent more time travelling than at their bungalow in the town of Carmel Cove. This was the longest they'd stayed at home all year, after returning in November to make plans for Christmas. When she'd visited her parents a few days earlier, even though her mother had tried to hide the map of the UK under the coffee table, Ruth had spotted the corner of it poking out. She knew another trip was imminent, despite her mother telling her they weren't planning one until the spring.

"We're fine. Your father is busy decorating the spare room. You know how much he hates sitting still. He's planning on putting up a few shelves in that room. We've got so many boxes of books in the garage. We've been here five years now. I told him it was about time we emptied them. You know what they say, unless you empty all the boxes after you've moved into a property, you're liable to put the house on the market if you don't."

"Really? I've not heard of that one. What colour are you painting it?"

"A coffee colour on the accent wall. Your father is also going to try his hand at hanging wallpaper for the first time after all these years."

"Good luck with that one. James and I attempted to do the same in our master bedroom. It was a disaster that I don't intend repeating anytime soon. When are you going away again?"

There, I've finally asked the question. Now let's see if she wriggles out of it.

"I told you, not until spring. Why do you persist in doubting me, Ruth?"

"Hmm...I wonder why that would be? Oh, maybe because you

3

have the travelling bug and can't stay in one place for more than a few months."

"Granted, if a little harshly put by what I'm picking up from your tone. Anyway, don't forget we have the wonderful function we want to attend at the weekend."

"How could I forget that? I can't say I'm looking forward to it myself, and yes, James and I were invited as well."

"Darling, how wonderful. We can all go together. Won't that be fun?"

"Super," Ruth replied, trying to keep her voice free from sarcasm.

She loved her mother dearly. She was a former doctor in the town, while her father used to be a renowned heart surgeon at Bristol Royal Infirmary, before they both hung up their stethoscopes over a year earlier. However, her mother had always been a socialite. Her wardrobe was full of glittery long dresses, rarely ever worn more than a handful of times.

"I sense some apprehension in your voice."

"No, not at all, Mum. I'm just cold, that's all. Do you think the function will still take place at the weekend if the weather persists?"

"I'm sure they'll have organised it in such a way as to compensate for what the weather has in store for us, they'd be foolish not to. We'll discuss it more later in the week. I'd better fly now. Your father will be demanding I feed him in between putting up the next roll of wallpaper. Don't forget the offer still stands. You can come and stay with us until the heating is fixed."

"Thanks for the offer, Mum, but hopefully that will be done in the next few hours. I'll speak soon."

Ruth hung up as James walked into the room carrying two steaming mugs of coffee which he placed on the coffee table in front of her.

"If you think it's cold in here, it's a darn sight worse in the kitchen."

"You should have turned on the gas oven while you were out there." She chuckled.

"Are you for real? Why waste money like that? Anyway, it would have taken over ten minutes to have heated up. I wasn't out there that long. Who was on the phone?"

"Mum. She's getting excited about the function at the weekend and has invited herself to tag along with us. Hope that's all right?"

James, ever the easy-going one, shrugged. "Fine by me. Can't say I'm thrilled to be going, are you?"

"Not really. I've admired the woman's writing for years, although I can't say I've ever had the inclination to meet her in person. I'm only doing this as a favour to Steven. He's invited all the members of the Amateur Dramatic club and their partners. I think he's organising the bash at the event along with the party organiser at the hotel. Apparently, she was feeling overwhelmed with all the demands put upon her by Ms. Bramley."

"Oh no, don't say she's going to turn out to be one of these diva types I've heard about and detested over the years?"

"Sounds like it." Ruth sipped at the warm liquid and wrapped both her hands around the mug.

James took his seat again and snuggled in close. Exchanging bodily warmth was the key to preventing them from turning into blocks of ice.

"The thought of dressing up in this weather isn't exactly filling me with glee."

Ruth nodded and pulled a face. "I know what you mean. I promised Steven I would wear a long dress for the occasion."

"What? You in a dress? Blimey, I hope Geraldine doesn't hear about that after you refusing to be a bridesmaid at her wedding because of that very reason."

Ruth gulped noisily. "Yikes, I never thought of that. Maybe I'm guilty of taking my hatred of dresses to extremes sometimes. If she gets to hear about it, I'll have to go down on bended knee and apologise."

"How's she coping now?"

"Since her husband was murdered, you mean? Fine, I thought she'd be wallowing in self-pity, but since the court case ended and Bradley's vile past was revealed, she appears to be getting on with her life."

"That's great to hear. I bet it'll take her a while before she can trust another man, though, right?"

"You'd think so. I wouldn't let another man near me if I were in her shoes, but she's had a few secret dates with someone."

"Who?"

"I can't believe you asked me that after I told you they were *secret* dates."

"Ah, right. I get you. When are you likely to find out who that person is?"

"Soon, I hope. I don't mind telling you that I'm a little concerned about her. What if this man arrived on the scene knowing how Bradley treated her?"

"What are you saying? That some men are attracted to a certain type of woman? A needy woman such as Geraldine? At least that's how she's always come across to me."

"Maybe. You hear so many dreadful stories of men homing in on vulnerable women who in their minds are ripe for the picking. How do we know this isn't what has happened to Geraldine?"

"If you're that concerned about her, you need to sit her down and tell her that."

"It would be different if she told me his name. At least then we could do a background check on him between us."

"Whoa! No more. I told you, after getting a warning from my boss that I can no longer help you. We're not allowed to carry out personal checks on people at the station anyway. You'd have to do that with the resources you use at the detective agency."

"Great. Thanks for your support." She sounded hurt—she wasn't really. She appreciated how many times he'd risked his career to supply her with information on an investigation she was dealing with. It was handy having a copper as a boyfriend when you were a private investigator for a living. Sometimes, on the rare occasion, that decision to lend a hand backfired, as it had on the last case she'd solved up at Carmel Cove Hall—the murder of Geraldine's husband, Bradley, only hours after they had tied the knot.

"I would if I could. You know I hate letting you down." He rested his head against hers.

"I know. I was only teasing. I need to buck my ideas up and start drawing on my own resources for the crimes I solve in the future and stop putting you in an awkward position."

He chuckled. "I'd appreciate that, and it would definitely get Inspector Littlejohn off my back. She's finding more and more to complain about at work, specifically when I complete a task for her."

Guilt flowed through her veins. "That's totally my fault. That woman has a genuine hatred for me. She's wrong to take it out on you, love. I'm sorry."

He kissed her forehead. "No need for you to apologise. I'll keep my head down at work for a while, see if that helps to keep her off my back. She's a hard woman, that one. Got some real personal issues if you ask me, not that I'm privy to her personal life. She pretty much keeps herself to herself at the station."

Her interest sparked. "I wonder what dark secrets she's trying to hide."

"I know that look. Don't even go there, Ruth. You leave well alone. She's not worth wrangling with. I think she'll come out on top every time."

Ruth raised an eyebrow. "Really? Maybe you're forgetting the number of crimes I've solved before she's even spoken to the first witness."

"No, I'm not. Lucky breaks most of them, you must admit that?"

"Some maybe. You can't say that about the last one I solved, though. That was all down to me seeing the crime scene photos for the very first time."

"Yep, and who supplied those photos? Muggins here, and I got punished for my stupidity as well."

"I told you, you should have taken photos of the damn photos. Instead, you brought the original pictures home for me to see."

"I know. I'm such a dunderhead at times."

"You might be occasionally."

He opened his mouth to speak.

She clamped her lips over his to silence his objection. "But I still love you."

"Just not enough to marry me," he grumbled.

She bashed her head against the back of the couch. "Give me strength. One day in the future, I promise. We're all right as we are now, aren't we? Why the rush to tie the knot?"

"Rush? Ten years together and you think I'm rushing you? Blimey, I've heard it all now. Most women would be falling over each other to hook a catch like me," he said, breaking the slight tension that had developed with a raucous laugh.

"In your dreams. That's what I love about you the most, your totally whacky sense of humour."

"Oi! Cheeky. I'll have you know there are several of the younger constables at work giving me the eye at the moment."

"Oh, there are, are there? Maybe you should give me their names, so I can warn them off."

"Not on your nelly! I've told them, in spite of their welcome advances, that I'm off the market and deeply in *lurve*."

"Oh, you have, have you? Pray tell me what their response has been to that?"

"They told me they're willing to accept the position for now, but made it clear that if ever things went wrong between us, they'd pounce straight away."

Ruth frowned and placed her gloved finger and thumb around her chin. "Is that so? Well, there's only one thing for it."

"What's that?" he asked like an eager puppy awaiting a ball to be thrown.

"You'd better tell me their names, and I'll go down the station to sort them out. No one flirts with my man and gets away with it."

"Nice to see you care."

They both laughed, content with one another's company in spite of the way they teased each other at times.

The phone rang again. Ruth answered it.

"Ruth, Ruth, is that you? I could do with your help at the hotel."

"Steven? Why? What on earth is going on?"

"She's arrived and is already doing my head in," he replied in his usual camp way.

"Who has? Not Jilly Bramley?"

"The one and only. Two whole days late, and she's demanding this, that and the other, making a mockery of the plans I've already put in place and what's to come. I'm going to be here until midnight every day between now and Saturday just undoing what I've already put in place. How could she possibly do that, to me of all people?"

Ruth cringed. Experience taught her what Steven could be like when things didn't go his way. He was an utter perfectionist. If Bramley had turned up and ripped into his ideas, she knew exactly how devastated he'd be about that. "Now calm down. I'm indisposed at the moment. I can come down there in a few hours if that will help?"

"What? A few hours? There's every chance I'd commit murder before you arrived. What's so important that you can't come right away? I'd drop anything and everything if you put out an emergency call for help, you know I would."

Ruth covered the mouthpiece of the phone and growled. "Damn, it's Steven. He's desperate for my help. It must be bad down there. He's just said he's liable to commit murder before long if things don't work out the way he planned them."

"Go. I'll stay here and wait for the engineer to come. There's no point both of us freezing to death. Ben will keep me company, won't you, boy?"

Ruth ruffled her constant companion's head as another bout of guilt ripped through her. "If you're sure?"

"Of course. Tell him you won't be long."

Ruth rubbed her nose against James'. "You're amazing. Thank you." Uncovering the phone, she said, "Steven, I'll be there in ten minutes, providing I can start the car. She's a pain in the rear on cold mornings."

Steven screeched. "Oh my, I can't thank you enough for this, Ruth."

"I'm sure when I get there I'll find you have everything under control and that you're panicking about nothing."

He grunted. "You couldn't be further from the truth, lovely. I'll see you soon." He ended the call before she could say anything else.

"Are you sure you don't mind?"

"Not at all. You go and warm up somewhere else, don't worry about us. I'm sure the engineer won't be long. The house will be all toasty and warm for you when you get back. Give me a ring if you get the chance, let me know how you're diddling."

She covered his mouth with hers in a lingering kiss that stirred something inside. *Maybe I could delay my trip for half an hour or so. I've already told Steven that the car is temperamental during the cold weather.* She sighed, resigned to leaving her man, never one to let a friend down when they were desperate for her help.

"Must fly. Thanks for understanding. I hope you don't turn to a block of ice before the engineer arrives."

"So do I. He'd better show up soon, otherwise I'm going to hit the roof."

"Be careful, you know how difficult it is to find an engineer willing to come out at the moment, due to them being snowed under with work."

James winced. "Was that a Freudian slip or an intentional pun?"

Ruth removed herself from the comfort of his arms and placed a gloved finger to her mouth. "That was a bad one, right? Maybe it's a good job I'm leaving."

He laughed. "You're not wrong there. Have fun."

"I doubt that very much. See you later," she called over her shoulder as she walked out of the room and went in search of her fur-lined flat boots. Wrapping an extra scarf around her neck, she collected her handbag and keys from the table and left via the front door. She crossed the fingers of one hand, inserted the key in Betty's ignition with the other and turned it. The car spluttered and died. "Oh crap, don't let me down now, girl. What if I promised you a run to warmer climates, such as a jaunt to Cornwall in the spring? Will you help me out then? Please, come on, do it for Mummy?"

She twisted the key again and laughed as her treasured car turned over. This was followed by a frustrated groan when Betty conked out a few seconds later.

"Give me strength. Betty, I need you. Steven needs me to come to his rescue. You know how much I detest letting my friends down. Please?"

She turned the key for the third time in as many minutes. As soon as Betty sparked into life, she pressed down hard on the accelerator, revving the engine until she felt Betty had enough life in her to take her on the trip.

She set off for the hotel which was only a ten-minute journey from home. The roads were a little icy in parts but nothing major. At least the snow the weatherman had forecast hadn't arrived yet.

The second she pulled up outside the hotel, Steven rushed out of the large front doors and down the steps to greet her. He hugged her tightly, forcing the air from her lungs. "Where's your coat? You'll freeze to death if you're not careful," she chastised him in a motherly fashion.

"I have bigger concerns to worry about than a teensy bit of cold. Blimey, you're wrapped up as though you're ready for an expedition to the Arctic. All that's missing is Ben to pull your sledge." He laughed loudly.

Ruth poked her tongue out at him and dug him in the ribs. "You can be such a wiseass at times. Come on, let's get inside. There you can use me and abuse me to your heart's content."

"Ooer, Missus. Now there's an offer I'd be foolish to refuse."

He linked his arm through hers, and together they ventured through the entrance. The lobby was decorated in silvers and blues of varying shades.

"This is beautiful, Steven. Did you do it?"

He nodded but didn't smile. "Isn't it? The party organiser rang in sick—correct that, her six-year-old son has a bout of tonsillitis and was rushed into hospital for some reason. Leaving me here to do all this. I've spent nearly two days getting this area decked out in this finery only for 'Diva Jilly' to trash it."

Ruth's head swivelled that fast her neck cracked. "What? Are you serious?"

"Yep. She hates it. End of. Told me to rip it down and start all over again."

She placed her gloved hand over his, which was still linked through her arm. "That's just downright rude. She has no right to do that, does she?"

"Apparently, her publicist, Sian Lawrence, a timid creature she is, likeable with it... Sorry, I digress. She told me not to take it personally and to call in reinforcements to get things changed ASAP. Which is all well and good, but blimey, what if I make the alterations and she hates those as well? What happens then? I put my heart and soul into this display."

"I can see you have, Steven. I'm so sorry. So has Jilly said what she wants?"

"That's just it. No, she hasn't. I've not been given a colour scheme to work with, nothing. And yet, if I repeated this display using a different colour palette, there's no telling if she'll like the results. I'm between a rock and a hard place, Ruth. That's why I called on you for help—well, that and to save my sanity. It's not that bad, is it?" He made a sweeping gesture with his arm around the room.

"No. I think it's absolutely perfect. I wouldn't change a thing and I'd categorically be thrilled if you provided a sumptuous display like this for any function I had in mind."

"And who, may I ask, are you?"

Ruth jumped when the voice boomed behind her. Steven's grip tightened on her. They glanced at each other out of the corner of their eyes before finally plucking up the courage to turn to face the new arrival.

"This is my good friend, Ruth. I've called her in to lend a hand," Steven spluttered nervously.

Ruth unhitched herself from his grasp and stared at the famous author who was the cause of Steven's anxiety. She removed the red glove from her right hand and offered it to the woman. Jilly Bramley's gaze dropped to Ruth's outstretched hand and then back up to her face.

"If you're here to help, then might I suggest that you damn well get on with it? You have a little over forty-eight hours to turn this place into something spectacular and to do away with this debacle."

Steven sucked in a breath beside her. Ruth placed a hand across his arm, preventing him from surging forward to scratch the woman's eyes out.

Ruth took the time to cool her anger in order to study the author. She looked well for her age — forty-eight — she'd read recently in one of the tabloid newspapers. Her clothes were definitely created by designers, as were her boots. Compared to the woman glaring at her, Ruth felt like a poorly dressed mannequin standing in the window of the local charity shop. She whipped off her hat and smoothed down her long red hair. That proved impossible to do because of the static energy within its length.

Jilly's eyes narrowed with every movement Ruth made. "I haven't got time to stand around here. I'm glad you've rallied reinforcements. May I suggest that you disrobe your excessive garments and get down to work?"

A guttural noise erupted from Ruth's throat. It was Steven's turn to try to restrain her. Before either of them could object further, Jilly swept away from them, her red, fifties-style dress swishing around her legs.

Ruth and Steven remained glued to the spot for what seemed like an eternity, neither of them finding the words to speak. Until finally, Ruth expelled a large breath. "What an utter…"

Steven raised his hands and covered his ears. "Please don't swear. You know how tender my ears are to such bad language. Although, I wouldn't blame you in the slightest if you did unleash a bucketload of vile expletives. I'd be tempted to join you if I thought I'd get away with it in God's eyes. Some people have that effect on you, don't they?"

"Don't they just? I was going to ask her what she found so distasteful, but she flounced away before I could summon up the right words. How do people put up with her?"

"Your guess is as good as mine. We'd better get to work. It's going to take us hours to tear this lot down."

"That's all well and good, but what are you going to replace it with at this late stage?"

Steven raised his arms out to the sides then dropped them heavily against his thighs. "I need to go to the town hall and source what's available."

Ruth sniggered, a wicked thought filtering into her mind.

Steven leaned in close. "I know that look when I see it. What are you planning, lady?"

"What if...you decked this place out in *The Sound of Music* set?"

Steven gasped. "I couldn't do that...or could I?" He placed his extended forefinger against his cheek as he thought. Then he sniggered and said, "I've got an even better idea."

"What are you up to?"

"What about *The Wizard of Oz*?"

Ruth doubled over, her laughter filling the vast space and rebounding off the walls. She stood upright and wiped the tears from her eyes. "You're a scream. I love it. Look, there's no way on earth we're going to be able to pull this off by ourselves. Why don't I ring the rest of the members of the club, see if they wouldn't mind coming down here and lending us a hand? Many hands and all that."

Steven flew at her, suffocating her in a bear hug. "Darling, what would I do without your devious mind to keep me company? What a super idea. You start ringing round while I begin tearing this lot down and packing it away."

"Hang on." She withdrew her phone from her pocket and shot a dozen or more photos from different angles of the room. "It's still a beautiful display that you can use in your portfolio, sweetheart, no matter what the Wicked Witch of the East says."

Steven laughed, his eyes glistening with tears as the colour rose in his cheeks. "You really are a friend to be treasured, Ruth. I'm not sure what I'd do without you fighting in my corner."

"You'd survive. I have little doubt about that. I'll sit over here and make the calls. I wonder if there's any chance of getting a coffee around here, the free variety. I'm aware of the prices they charge from when I treated Mum to afternoon tea here last year."

He winked at her. "You do what you've got to do. Let me try and do a deal for us. There's no reason why they shouldn't give us a cup. After all, we're decorating their hotel for them free of charge."

"Exactly." Ruth headed towards the plush red seats in the reception area and slipped out of her outerwear now that the ice in her veins had started to thaw a little. She then set about calling the other members of the Am-Dram club. Twenty minutes later, the other three members all bounced through the door together.

"Wow, this place is amazing. What a fantastic job you've done, Steven," Hilary, the doctor's receptionist gushed.

"I echo that. You're such a talented man, Steven. I bet Jilly and her entourage will be blown away when they see what you've created," Gemma, the local hairdresser chipped in.

Lynn Harris, who helped out at the detective agency now and then as a volunteer to break the monotony of being a housewife, spun around, her mouth open at the extravaganza on view. "It's phenomenal. Well done you, Steven."

All the praise overwhelmed Steven. He collapsed in a heap and buried his head in his hands. Ruth left her coffee and rushed across the room to assist him. The other three women all stared at each other, puzzled expressions etched on their faces.

"Ruth, what's going on? Steven, are you all right?" Hilary asked, trying to pull him to his feet.

"He'll be fine. I didn't mention why we need your help over the phone because I wanted to see what your reaction was when you got down here and saw all this for yourselves. It's stunningly beautiful, isn't it?"

The three women frowned and nodded.

"Apparently, it's *not*. Jilly Bramley hates it and has demanded that Steven tears all his good work down. That's why he's beside himself."

"No! How could she be so heartless? What does she want then if this isn't good enough?" Lynn asked, reaching out and rubbing a comforting hand up and down Steven's back.

Ruth tugged at Steven's arm, encouraging him to stand. His tearful eyes tore at her heart. She hugged him hard. "See, we're all behind you, Steven. Don't let that dreadful woman win."

He sniffled and wiped his nose on the sleeve of his jumper. "I'm trying not to. When you put every ounce of energy into a project and someone comes along and disses it in one second flat, it's extremely hard to swallow."

"What will you do?" Gemma asked, perplexed.

"We have to destroy all this and create something new," Ruth said, dejectedly.

The others gasped. Ruth motioned for them to come closer. They all wrapped an arm around each other and leaned in, their heads almost touching in the circle they formed.

"Steven and I have come up with a plan, but we need you guys to lend a hand to pull it off before Saturday."

"What? Two days to get this place stripped and dressed again? Is that within the realms of possibility, Ruth?" Hilary asked, breaking the circle.

Gemma pulled her back into the fold. "Why don't you listen for a change instead of standing there thinking up excuses why things can't be done?"

"I refute that. I said nothing of the sort," Hilary growled back, annoyed.

"Ladies, please, for goodness' sake, can't you put your petty squabbling aside for a few days? Steven needs us," Ruth chastised them.

"I agree if she does," Gemma replied.

Hilary nodded. "If I have to."

"Right, I'm glad to hear it. This is the plan we've come up with but we're going to need your help to pull it off in the time left available to us," Ruth whispered conspiratorially.

"I'm dying to hear, although I can't see anything but redoing what you've created here, Steven." Lynn smiled and gave Steven an extra squeeze.

"Thank you, all of you. Your kind words have lessened the load on my heart. I can't thank you enough for volunteering to do this with me and Ruth. I'll be forever in your debt."

"A little overdramatic there, Steven. Friends always come together when the chips are down. Listen up, girls, this is what we intend to put on for her ladyship."

"Go on, we're eager to hear," Gemma urged when Ruth cleared her throat to tell them the plan.

"We're going to turn this place into a set from *The Wizard of Oz*!"

The three newcomers stepped back from the circle and stared at Ruth.

Finally finding her voice, Lynn said, "My goodness, whatever would Ms. Bramley say about that?"

Ruth shrugged. "It'll serve her right. She should have treated Steven better. It's not as if she's paying him for his time. He spent what? Three days decorating this area alone this week?"

Steven nodded as fresh tears bulged. "That's right."

"Well, with our help we can make this place look stunning and wipe the floor with Ms. Ultra-Famous Author Extraordinaire at the same time. What do you say, girls?"

"Count me in," Lynn oozed, her excitement evident. "I love the idea of getting one over on someone willing to rip a person's hard work to shreds the way she has. Poor Steven. Let's do it for our dear friend."

"Hilary, Gemma?" Ruth asked, turning to face the other two women.

"I don't know. You know what I'm like. I hate causing anyone any kind of pain," Hilary complained.

"Get away with you. What about the pain she's caused Steven for no reason? Look at this place," Gemma chastised Hilary harshly. She gestured around the room with her arm. "No one in their right mind would diss this stunning display. The woman must have a screw loose."

"I agree. No normal person would tear someone's efforts apart like she has. She deserves her comeuppance. Come on, Hils, say you'll lend us a hand?" Ruth said.

Hilary let out a huge sigh. "If I have to. I'm telling you now that it doesn't sit well with me and that I'm only doing this for Steven's sake. He looks crushed, and I hate anyone feeling that way at the hands of others."

Ruth applauded her statement. "That's my girl. Let's split up. Gemma, do you want to go to the town hall with Steven to source the new decorations? The rest of us will remain here and pack all this lot away."

"Sounds like a good idea," Steven replied, fist-bumping Gemma.

Ruth couldn't have been prouder of her group of friends. They'd always stepped up to the mark in the past but, in Ruth's eyes they'd gone far beyond anything they'd done before in this task. She just hoped they would be able to pull it off before Saturday. She really didn't care what Jilly's reaction would be when she saw the final results either.

"Let's do this. The Am-Dram club to the rescue."

2

It turned out to be two days of bedlam. Everyone pitched in when they had spare time, but most of the onus to get the hotel's reception area redecorated within forty-eight hours lay solely on Steven's and Ruth's shoulders. Steven, who was a caretaker at the local school, had even booked time off work to carry out the task for the ungrateful author. Ruth arranged to have her business calls diverted to her mobile; therefore, if any calls came in to the office she was able to answer any enquiries right away and still lend her friend the assistance he needed to pull off the mammoth mission.

On numerous occasions, when things had started to get on top of him, Ruth had guided him over to the seating area to force him to take a break. His stress levels were borderline out of control.

"Whatever would I do without you, Ruth? You've been a godsend these past few days. I'll never be able to repay you for the work you've put in around here."

"Nonsense, love, it's what friends are for. It's not as if I'm inundated with work at the moment. It's been an absolute pleasure to help out a friend in need and to do something different for a change."

"I just have to blow up about a hundred yellow balloons and dot them around, and then I think we're done."

"It looks amazing. Thank goodness Jilly's publicist and agent have managed to help us out by keeping her away from the area. By the time she sees it for herself, it'll be too late to change it all again."

They both laughed.

"I know my name is going to be mud, but it might teach her to be more appreciative in the future when someone busts a gut to get something looking nice for her."

"I doubt it. We live in hope, though. Anything else for me to do?"

"I don't think so now. We need to tidy away a few of the boxes, and that's us done."

"Okay, I'll do that and go in search of Sian, see if we can get her approval at least before we leave."

"Good idea." Steven glanced at his watch. "We have to be back here for the evening's event at seven, although I'd like to be around before then if it's possible. If I don't fall asleep in the bath, that is. Crikey, we haven't stopped. What an achievement, eh, Ruth?" He smiled as he surveyed the room, obviously chuffed with their efforts.

"It's brilliant, there's no doubting that." *But then so was the first display, and the diva hated that.* "I'll be back in a jiffy."

Ruth strode through the hotel's hallways in search of Sian. She wandered into the dining room. Neither she nor Steven had any dealings with decorating this area, and to be honest, it showed. Still, if Diva Jilly hadn't spat her dummy out of the pram, this room could have, and would have, looked stunning. Instead, it was now presented as the Plain Jane room of the hotel in comparison to the foyer. Sian entered the room from a door on the left. She was carrying a tray with a pile of cutlery and napkins.

"Hello, Sian, I was looking for you. You seem as stressed as me and Steven. Are you?"

She placed the tray on one of the tables and sighed. "She's a hard task master, I'll give you that. I've barely slept all week because my mind refuses to shut down."

"I'm not sure I could be around her eight to ten hours a day, that's for sure. I admire your resilience."

"Resilience or stupidity? I'm not sure which." A glimmer of a smile pulled at Sian's weary features.

"Why do it? Why be around someone who is downright rude and so ungrateful all the time?"

"I've been with her for the past ten years. I suppose it's hard to break that regime. Deep down, I think she appreciates what people do for her. I suppose she believes that the general public expects her to have a certain air about her, especially at functions such as this. You mustn't forget that she's a very talented author, who works hard on her novels. I've often seen a light on in her bedroom at two or three in the morning, Jilly perfecting a scene she's written during the day that hasn't sat well with her."

"Ah, the traits of a perfectionist. I've heard about people like that. I'm one of those people who like things in a certain order but I wouldn't necessarily call myself a perfectionist. Does that affect the way she deals with people, do you think?"

"You mean what she's put you and your friend through, changing the reception area?"

"Yes."

"She can be the harshest critic. Again, maybe that's because she's such a perfectionist." She leaned in and whispered, "Between you and me, I thought your friend did an absolutely fabulous job."

"So did I. I'm surprised he didn't walk when she said she hated it. I think I would have if I'd been in his shoes."

"And yet you stuck around to help him put things right—not that there was anything wrong with the way it was in the first place."

"That's me all over. I could never let a friend down, not when they need me most. What about her agent? Megan, is it?"

"That's right. Well, Megan knows Jilly of old. She's been with her since Jilly released her first book. She's a huge admirer of her work."

"I am, too. I think I've read every novel she's ever written, up until last year. For the past eighteen months or so, I've been too busy trying to get my business off the ground to have any real spare time to call my own."

"It must be difficult being self-employed these days. What line of business are you in, if you don't mind me asking?"

"I run a detective agency, for my sins."

Sian frowned and folded her arms. "A detective agency? Are you linked to the police? Or am I missing something?"

"Okay, I'm what's commonly known as a private investigator."

Sian's eyes widened, and her mouth dropped open for a moment. Eventually, she found her voice to ask, "Wow, what type of things do you investigate?"

"Anything and everything. Let's just say I can't afford to be fussy. I have bills to pay like every other inhabitant in this town."

"How exciting. Give me an example of the types of crimes you've investigated recently?"

Ruth could tell the timid woman in her thirties was genuinely interested in her work. "Well, generally, I'm instructed by clients to follow their spouses, to see what type of thing they're getting up to."

"Men. Aren't they the pits at times?"

Ruth chuckled. "I have to say women are more at fault than men these days."

Sian gasped. "Get away! Wow, who would've thought that?"

"I'd probably put the statistics at sixty-forty."

"Which begs the question why people go through the expense of having a wedding if all they're going to do is cheat on their partner after the rings are exchanged. Shameful behaviour."

"Definitely. I suppose it's the world we live in now. Most of the couples I deal with end up getting divorced. However, occasionally, it does make a couple realise that the grass isn't always greener on the other side and they stay together, even if it means they have to go through a number of counselling sessions."

"Glad to hear it. Doesn't that sort of thing get boring after a while?"

Ruth inclined her head. "Not really. You'd think all the cases would be the same, but they can vary significantly. I do have some spicier cases thrown into the mix now and again."

"Ooh, such as? Tell me more?"

Ruth chuckled. "The odd murder or attempted murder. I had a case only last year where the husband had snipped the brake lines on his wife's car. Luckily, she came off the road on a sharp bend, and the car ended up headfirst in a haystack."

"Wow, she must've been scared witless. I'd be out of my mind with worry and unable to drive a car again. How did you find out it was the husband?"

"Pure detective work. One of the locals contacted me to say they'd overheard the husband talking with a friend about the incident at the local pub. He thought it was strange that the husband was laughing about the 'mishap'."

"What a callous so-and-so. Was he arrested?"

"Yes, and sentenced to six years in prison. He'll be out in three years. The wife has since changed her name and left the area. Said she couldn't face seeing him again after betraying her like that."

"I don't blame her. I think I'd do the same. So, it can be an exciting career then, is that what you're telling me?"

"It can also be heartbreaking at the same time. I won't go into details but I was asked to investigate my friend's husband's death—or murder as it turned out—in July of last year. The thing is, the murder happened on their wedding day."

"No way! Blimey, I'd love to hear the details on that one when we have more time."

"We'll sit down and chat when we have a spare minute. It was a horrendous few days trying to work out who the killer was."

"I'm confused. Wouldn't the police be involved in a major case such as that?"

"They were. The local inspector is, how shall I put this? As much use as a chocolate teapot."

Sian chortled. "I'm with you. Makes you wonder how people like that sleep at night, doesn't it?"

"It certainly does. Okay, we'd better get on. What I wanted was to get your opinion on what Steven and I have been doing for the past few days. Do you have time to take a peek?"

"Of course. I did take a sneaky look last night and thought it was wonderful."

Ruth cringed. "Does that mean Jilly has seen it as well?"

"No. I've intentionally kept her away from the area. More to keep her stress levels to a minimum than anything else."

"Thank goodness. What do you think her reaction is going to be when she sees it? It was the best we could come up with in such a short space of time and with a limited amount of set to work with."

Shrugging, Sian said, "She'd be foolish if she didn't like it. Honestly, there's no telling with her. I've had experience over the years of her liking the things that I found distasteful and hating the things I'd think should appeal to her. She's a devil to please sometimes. Let's go and have a gander."

They walked side by side through the hotel and back to the entrance lobby.

Sian's smile was as wide as a river. "I think it's simply gorgeous and very inventive, but that's my take on it."

"But do you think her ladyship will appreciate it?" Ruth asked, crossing her fingers behind her back as she anticipated Sian's response.

"Well, if she doesn't, I suppose we'll all hear about it pretty soon." She surprised Ruth by applauding her and Steven. "Well done, the pair of you. What you've pulled off is simply amazing. Maybe you've missed your vocation in life."

The three of them laughed.

"It was mostly down to Steven. He was the brains behind the task. I just added the brawn here and there."

"I was just coming over to congratulate you myself," David Strong, the hotel manager said when he crossed the lobby to join them. "I'm sorry my member of staff let you down."

Ruth let out a relieved breath. Steven yelped with joy and hugged her hard.

"We did it," Steven shouted. He danced around on the spot, which made them all chuckle.

Ruth slapped his upper arm. "You can be such an idiot at times. A word of caution, don't get too excited. Jilly hasn't seen it yet."

"Did you have to throw a virtual bucket of water over my good mood?" Steven replied.

"I must fly. I still have some preparations to do in the ballroom." Sian waved at them and dismissed herself.

Ruth felt a twinge of guilt as she watched the woman scurry away. She should have offered to help for at least half an hour, except time was getting on and she ached all over and was longing for a hot bath to soothe her pain.

"Go on. I know it takes you women an eternity to get ready. You shoot off. I'll finish blowing up the balloons before I go home."

"If you're sure? What time shall we arrange to meet later?"

"What about six forty-five? That gives you two hours to soak your weary bones and dress in all your finery. You are wearing that dress I sorted out for you, aren't you?"

"I am. It's hanging up in my wardrobe ready to slip on later. I can't say I'm not apprehensive about wearing it, but a promise is a promise."

"It is. I knew you wouldn't let me down. I picked out the best dress we had in stock at the town hall props department. I'm quite envious, if you must know."

Ruth laughed. "You should have worn it yourself, turned up as an alter ego. That way Jilly wouldn't know who to come after if she doesn't like the display."

Steven covered his mouth with his hand. "Well, get you and your bright ideas."

"No! You wouldn't?"

Steven winked and shooed her out of the front door. "See you later, darling."

She started Betty on the fourth attempt, promising to get her serviced at the earliest opportunity, and drove home. Whipping off her coat and scarf, she smiled as the warmth of the house comforted her.

James appeared in the lounge doorway. "All fixed. Nice to feel some heat around here again. I put the water on, so you'll have hot water for your bath."

She sashayed towards him. "What a treasure you are. Want to come up and scrub my back?"

"I'll be up shortly. I was about to take Ben for a walk."

"Thanks, I was wondering whether I'd be able to fit a walk in before we leave. The place looks fabulous, by the way, thanks for asking," she teased.

"There was never any doubt, not with you guys putting the work in. Has the diva seen it?"

"Not yet, although her publicist thought it was amazing. She seems a lovely girl. What on earth she's doing working for that tyrant, I'll never know."

"Each to their own. She obviously likes the woman, otherwise she wouldn't be at her beck and call twenty-four-seven, would she?"

"True. I hate the thought of a nice person such as Sian being treated appallingly, though. I'm glad I'm self-employed. Crikey, how many times have I uttered those words over the years?"

He laughed. "More times than I care to mention. See you in a little while."

They parted with a kiss. She watched James and Ben disappear into the kitchen then walked up the stairs to the bathroom. A few minutes later, she was reclining in a bath full of bubbles, the tension in her shoulders and muscles gently easing. After a while, she heard the back door close and the sound of Ben bounding up the stairs. He poked his head around the bathroom door, searching for her.

"Here, boy." She scooped up a handful of bubbles, waited until he was about a foot away from her and blew them towards him. He ended up with a small clump on the tip of his nose. He sneezed and swept a paw over his snout to dislodge them. Ruth sniggered. "That'll teach you to be so nosy. Maybe you'll give me some privacy next time I decide to have a bath."

He moaned and lay down on the bathmat beside her. James tapped on the door.

"Come in. My modesty is well and truly hidden. Do you want to have a bath after me? Or are you opting for a shower?"

"You know me, I'd rather jump in and out of a steaming shower than soak in a tub and end up prune-like."

"There's nothing wrong with looking like a prune now and again. I suppose I'd better get a wriggle on. I promised Steven I would push the boat out for the event this evening and go all out with the makeup et cetera."

"Huh, that's charming. You'll do it for Steven but you refuse to do it for me."

"Don't give me that little-boy-hurt look. Since when does a special occasion such as this grand affair rear its head around here?"

"What about birthdays and anniversaries, don't they count?"

"You mean the anniversary of our first date?" She cringed, realising what she'd said and expecting some form of witty retort about marriage in return.

"I could be talking about a wedding anniversary if only you'd give me a chance."

She slipped farther into the water until her head was buried. When she emerged, James had taken the hint and left the bathroom. *Damn, does that mean he's in a strop? That's all I need for the evening ahead.*

After another five minutes' soak, Ruth pulled out the plug and dried herself with the fluffy white towel she'd placed on the heated rail. Walking into the bedroom, she snuck up behind James who was standing in front of the mirror combing his hair with a towel draped around his hips. "Are you angry with me?"

He turned to face her, frowning. "No, should I be? Oh, you mean the jibe about the wedding again?"

"It tugs on my heart every time you mention it. As though your intent is to use it as a form of torture."

"Nonsense. Half the time I'm teasing you."

"And the other half?" she asked, pouting.

"The other half I ask you in the hope that one day I'll break down your barrier and you'll finally agree to walk down the aisle with me. We're not getting any younger, and your biological clock is ticking away."

"Gee, thanks. Well, insults like that are hardly going to alter my mind, are they?" she said light-heartedly.

"Whatever. Okay, I'll get dressed and be out of your hair in a few minutes."

"Are you wearing your tux?"

"Will it help to change your mind?" He raised an expectant eyebrow.

"Nice try, buster. You know how handsome you always look in your tux and the effect it has on me. You never know, one of these days I'll surprise you and say yes."

"Are you telling me that you're weakening, finally coming around to the idea?"

She reached for her watch on the chest of drawers. "Oh my, is that the time? It's going to take me an hour or so to get into that dress."

"Ever one for avoiding the subject." He walked away from her, his shoulders slumped in resignation.

While her heart ached because of the pain she sometimes inflicted upon him, she knew, deep down, that she still wasn't ready to commit, no matter how much she loved him. It left her wondering as she dried herself and put on her makeup, if she was in a minority. Were there other women out there dragging their feet regarding walking down the aisle? She also wondered if there were, how long their partners were prepared to wait before they went in search of someone else.

The dress, black and long, was covered in sequins that scratched her skin when she finally got around to slipping it on. "Ouch! Is it any wonder I don't wear dresses or skirts?" Once the torturous ordeal was completed, she studied her reflection and nodded approvingly. "You'll do. You scrub up nicely for a thirty-five-year-old bird, soon to be thirty-six."

Distracted, she neglected to hear James approaching her from behind and jumped when he placed a hand around her waist and nuzzled her neck. Her hair was pulled to one side, revealing a bare patch on the left which his lips homed in on. She moaned softly, enjoying his loving touch. Then she bounced back to reality with a bump and slapped his hand away.

"Don't go starting any funny business. We'll be late."

"Five minutes won't hurt."

"Ha, if you could have witnessed the struggle I had getting into this dress, you'd realise what an idiotic suggestion that is."

"Oh well, it was worth a try. Does this mean we're good to go?"

She spun around and her heart skipped several beats. "You look amazing. You should wear that suit more often."

He tilted his head back and laughed. "If I turned up like this to go to the pub, the landlord would be on the phone to the asylum within seconds."

"You know what I mean. All right, what I should have said was perhaps we're both guilty of not making the appropriate effort, agreed?"

"Maybe, although I'd never fully admit to that. I think I put more effort into this relationship than any of my mates do with theirs, not that it gets me anywhere."

"I appreciate what we have, James, never doubt that. Perhaps I'm scared that if I commit fully, everything will implode. Why change things when we're at our happiest?"

"I hear what you're saying. I promise not to nag you again in the foreseeable future, how's that?"

They shared a brief kiss. Ruth topped up her lipstick and picked up the sparkly clutch purse Steven had supplied to go with the dress. "Deal. We'd better get down there before Steven throws a hissy fit. Let's hope all our efforts over the past few days are worth it and that Jilly finally appreciates what we've done for her. Put it this way, if she doesn't, then I'll sweep Steven aside and swing for her myself."

"I'm sure everything will go according to plan. Come on, the taxi is due any minute now."

"What about Ben? He'll need feeding. I wonder if Mrs Sanders will pop in later to check he's all right."

"Already taken care of. She said she'll bring her Kindle with her and sit with him for an hour or two. No doubt she'll spoil him in the process."

"Oh heck, I hope she doesn't ply him with too many treats, otherwise his diet will be in jeopardy."

"One night won't harm him. I'll take him for an extra run tomorrow. He can work off the excess pounds he's likely to gain then."

A horn blasted in the street beneath their window.

"Damn, the taxi driver is early. Where did I put my shoes?"

James dipped down on the other side of the bed and held her black evening sandals by the straps.

"Thank goodness."

They rushed down the stairs, patted Ben on the head and sent him to his bed, slipped on their shoes and coats and left the house. During the journey, her mother rang.

"Mum, how's it going?"

"I'm sorry, love. We're not going to make it," her mother replied, her voice as croaky as a toad. "We've both got the flu—at least, that's what it feels like."

"How awful. You were looking forward to this evening. Go to bed. Hope you're better soon."

"We're in bed now; we ache all over. Speak soon, dear."

Ruth ended the call and placed her phone in her bag. "Poor Mum and Dad have the flu."

"Damn, they were looking forward to this evening."

"Never mind. They're better off home in bed." She snuggled up to him, linking her arm through his. "Looks like it'll just be you and me tonight, hon."

"Sounds perfect to me."

3

*W*hen they arrived at the hotel, Steven was standing on the steps, pacing up and down, waiting for them.

"Does he seem more anxious than normal, or is that me over-thinking things?" James said, leaning over to peer through the side window.

"It doesn't look good, I must admit."

"I'll pay the driver, you go on ahead."

Steven spotted them draw up and raced down the steps. He yanked the door open and held out his hand to aid Ruth from the car. "Oh, thank goodness. I knew you wouldn't let me down, although I was beginning to wonder where you were."

Smoothing down her dress and trying to balance on her heels at the same time, Ruth asked, "What's wrong? I told you we'd be here at six forty-five."

"Yes, you did. By my watch it's two minutes after that."

"Is that all? You know what a terrible timekeeper I am."

"It slipped my mind. You look absolutely fabulous, by the way."

Ruth smiled. "So do you. Are the others here yet?"

"No. Hopefully they're on their way."

After paying the driver, James joined them. He shook hands with

Steven. "Why don't we go inside where it's warmer, guys? I'm eager to see the display."

The two men stood either side of Ruth and linked arms with her as they walked up the steps. Steven even lifted her dress a few inches so she didn't fall flat on her face in his haste to get them inside.

"Wow, okay, this is very different," James said, glancing around the bright-yellow set. "What has Jilly said?"

"She still hasn't seen it. Her publicist and agent both love it, though, so I'm hoping Ruth and I have nailed it this time."

The main doors opened, and in swept the rest of the Am-Dram club with their respective partners.

After the greetings were out of the way, Gemma gave a low whistle. "Guys, I have to tell you, I never thought you'd pull it off. It's amazing."

"Oh ye of little faith," Ruth replied with a tut. "We worked damn hard to get this place ready in time. We only finished a few hours ago."

Before anyone else in the group could compliment Ruth and Steven on their achievements, a bloodcurdling screech echoed around the room. Ruth rolled her eyes at James, fearful of what she might find when she turned around.

He gripped her hand and whispered, "She doesn't seem happy."

"Crap."

Ruth tried to latch on to Steven who was just out of her reach. The colour swiftly drained from his face, and he was trembling as he stared at Jilly.

Mortified, he walked towards her. She took two steps forward and slapped him hard around the face. He shrieked in horror and held his hand over the cheek Jilly had struck.

Ruth wasn't about to let Jilly treat her dear friend in such an abhorrent way. Despite James clawing at her arm, she flew forward and confronted the woman with a pointed finger close to her face. "Now listen here, Ms. Bramley. There is no call for you to treat Steven like that, not after all he's done for you. Without payment I might add. I wonder if your guests realise what an ungrateful minx you are. Steven and I have worked our butts off for two solid days, erecting another beautiful display because you hated the previous one, which was regarded as absolutely stunning by everyone but you. How dare you rip into people the way you do? You're nothing special. Yes, I've been a lifelong admirer of your work, but after meeting and dealing with you first-hand, that's going to stop, I can assure you. Lady, you need to remove that huge chip off your shoulder and start being grateful for the work people do to help make you look good in the public eye." Ruth's heart rate quadrupled in those feisty few moments. She inhaled a steadying breath and stared at the woman she'd just brought down a peg or two on behalf of her friend.

Jilly's highly made-up face turned a deep shade of beetroot. She glared at Ruth, her eyes narrowing and widening at regular intervals. "Who the hell do you think you are, lady?"

Ruth raised her hand, preventing the author from speaking further. "As I've already stated, I'm a long-time admirer of your work. Answer me one question: have you ever in your life praised anyone around you for doing an excellent job?"

Jilly's gaze drifted to Sian and Megan standing alongside her, their heads dropped, unable to make eye contact with their boss. "Ladies? Have I ever not thanked you for a job well done? Or not appreciated the work you do for me?"

Neither Megan nor Sian spoke, their gazes still directed at the floor.

Ruth had to stifle the urge to pump the air with her fist in jubilation. This was totally unlike her to make a show of someone in public, let alone a famous author. Maybe she was more exhausted than she first thought, and it was tiredness that had caused her to react the way she had.

"Well, thanks, ladies. I suppose your silence speaks volumes. You'll both be seeking new jobs come the morning." Jilly turned on her slender heels, her stunning gold lamé skin-tight evening dress rustling as she moved away from the crowd.

Ruth gasped and placed a hand over her mouth.

Steven rushed forward and threw an arm around her shoulder and pecked her on the cheek. "You go, girl. I've never seen you so worked up before."

Ruth's eyes watered, and she reached out to grasp his hand. "What have I done? My God, I've cost these women their jobs, all because I couldn't control my big mouth."

Sian and Megan both shook their heads.

Megan smiled and said, "You've done nothing of the sort. She often flies off the handle at us. She sees us as whipping girls most of the time, lashes out for no reason and fires us more times than we can shake a stick at. She'll go back to her room and lick her wounds for half an hour and then emerge as if nothing has happened. Please, don't worry. You had a right to speak to her that way after the work you've put in around here. I'm sorry she doesn't appreciate it. We both admire what you've created; it's a truly wondrous display. I'm sure the other guests will be thrilled by it too, when they arrive. Talking of which, they're due any second now, and we still have a few things to finalise, so if you'll excuse me and Sian, we'd better make sure everything else is tickety-boo."

Ruth smiled and exhaled a relieved sigh as the two women left the group. Her friends took it in turns to hug Ruth, praising her for speaking up the way she had. Then it was James' turn. He stepped forward and placed a finger under her chin. Their gazes met for a few moments before his mouth covered hers. The rest of the group cheered. Ruth pulled away from him, her cheeks the warmest part of her.

"I'm so proud of you. You gave her a few home truths that others should have given her a long time ago. Don't feel bad for speaking out, Ruth. Not when you were right. The cheek of that woman. I feel sorry for Megan and Sian having to put up with her temper tantrums all the time."

"Thank you for your support, everyone. You all know how out of character that was for me. It's Steven I feel sorry for, all his hard work shot down in flames by that evil woman. Just who does she think she is?"

"Forget about her. Why don't we find the bar and get ourselves a drink," James suggested, holding her hand firmly in his.

"Really? You still want to stay? I was erring on the side of leaving.

Why should we pay tribute to the woman? Watch her bask in the glory she *doesn't* deserve?"

"I'm inclined to agree with you," Steven piped up.

"If you leave now, there's only going to be one winner—her! Don't let her have the satisfaction. I think we should hang around and make her suffer. Cause her to feel guilty for the way she's reacted and for the people she's deliberately upset," James replied, a twinkle sparkling in his eye.

Before Ruth could respond, Sian came rushing back into the hotel's foyer. "Oh Lordy, will this day ever end?"

"What's wrong now? Has she run out of her favourite toothpaste?" Ruth asked.

"No. It's far worse than that. One of the band members has been struck down by a mystery illness. I need to call an ambulance. Where on earth am I going to find a replacement drummer at this late stage?"

Ruth turned to face James and raised an eyebrow.

Reading her mind, he shook his head adamantly. "No way. Not in a million years."

"What's this?" Sian asked, her brow furrowing a little.

"James used to be a drummer in a band a few years ago," Ruth replied, hanging on to James' arm in case he got the urge to flee.

"Would you, please? There's no way I'll find someone else who is able to step in this late in the day," Sian pleaded, her hands clasped in a begging pose.

"Damn you, Ruth. When was the last time I played the drums? It's been at least five years since you forced me to sell my drum kit."

"Only because we needed the room. It's like riding a bike, isn't it? You'll remember as soon as the music begins to play, won't you? Isn't that how it works?"

He tutted and shook his head. "Er...not exactly. What if the piece of music leads with a rendition on the drums? What the heck do I do then?"

"Please, James, do it for me?"

"And what's in it for me?" he asked, pouncing on the opportunity.

She rolled her eyes and gritted her teeth. He was forcing her into a corner, and as it stood, there was no way out. "All right, we'll have a trial engagement."

The group whooped with joy as the happy couple kissed.

James pulled away and winked. "I knew you'd succumb to my charms one day."

She swiped his arm. "Get away with you. Go, you'd better get ready."

Sian smiled broadly. "You're a lifesaver. Let me call the ambulance, and I'll take you through and introduce you to the other members of the band. They're a nice bunch, so you should fit in. I can't thank you enough for coming to the rescue." She left the group and used her mobile to call the ambulance. She returned a few minutes later and whisked James away.

"Let's hope I haven't dropped him in it. I can understand his hesitation at not wanting to help the Wicked Witch of the East," Ruth announced to the others.

"He'll be fine. Someone mentioned finding the bar?" Hilary asked with a grin. "I could do with a G&T. I wonder if they've got any special gins on offer. My tastes have definitely altered in the last year or so. The ones I've sampled recently have been superb. I think my favourite has to be the salted caramel flavour. I discovered it at Lidl last week. I'm ashamed to say that I've polished off two whole bottles in ten days."

"Ooh, that sounds absolutely divine. Let's go and see, Hils." Steven tucked his arm through Hilary's and set off.

Hilary's husband, Denis the butcher, tutted at his wife's confession and followed close behind them.

The rest of them walked into the banqueting suite that looked a poor relation to the foyer Ruth and Steven had spent days creating. "Maybe this will be more to the evil witch's liking," Ruth muttered snarkily.

Gemma nudged her elbow. "I doubt it. I'm so proud of the way you spoke out. The rest of us would have stood back and taken it."

"I had to. Steven was ready to commit murder after she lambasted the other display he'd painstakingly whipped up. No one has the right to condemn someone's hard work in that way; it doesn't matter what circles they move in. Decent manners cost nothing, that's what Mum always instilled in me."

"I agree. Let's forget about it, set it aside and have a good time. Steven seems to have accepted it now. Thank heavens James stepped in at the last minute. Can't wait to see what type of ring he buys you."

Ruth laughed. "Knowing how tight he is, it'll probably be one he picks up from a charity shop."

"What? He wouldn't dare? Maybe he's got a ring hanging around that was his grandmother's, bless her soul."

"Maybe. We've never discussed it before. I can't believe I finally said yes." She leaned in and whispered, "Is it the done thing to have an engagement that lasts a decade?"

Gemma's eyes widened. "You wouldn't dare do that to him, would you?"

Ruth sniggered. "It would serve him right for cornering me like that."

"What's everyone having?" Steven asked, propping up the bar.

They all put in their orders.

"I'll have a vodka and orange, please, Steven. I wonder if James will be allowed to have a drink on stage with him. Ha, on stage, hark at me."

"I'll check," Denis said, going in search of the band.

"The punters are starting to arrive now," Hilary pointed out.

Steven withdrew some money from his wallet and threw it onto the bar. "Mine's a G&T. I must dash. I'm dying to see what people's reactions are."

The group laughed as they watched him race back to the hotel foyer. He glanced over his shoulder once he got there, grinning like a crazy person, and gave them a thumbs-up.

"I'm so pleased for him. He deserves all the praise he's about to receive after the blood, sweat and tears he's shed this week," Ruth said, her heart almost bursting at the seams.

Gemma flung an arm over her shoulder and pulled her in for a hug. "Don't forget you had a hand in it, too."

"I know, but I was only doing as I was instructed. He's a very clever man. Maybe his work ethic has surprised me this week. I think I might've been guilty of taking him for granted over the years."

Gemma nodded. "Perhaps we've all been a little guilty about that."

Hilary handed Ruth and Gemma their drinks. "Aren't all talented people treated the same way? I don't mean that disrespectfully. I'm just saying that people probably expect good things from the talented few amongst us, without realising the efforts behind their talents. Oh crumbs, listen to me. Did that come out as a lot of gobbledygook?"

"Not at all. It's basically what I said about taking someone for granted. Once someone shows a particular talent for achieving something, they're expected to maintain their high standards. I suppose I didn't realise until working with Steven this week, the amount of effort constantly needed to pull off something of this magnitude. I tell you what, if ever he turned his back on the Am-Dram club, we'd be up the creek."

"I get you. Maybe we can throw him some kind of thank-you party when all this has died down, to show him how much we appreciate him," Hilary suggested.

Ruth squealed. "What an excellent idea! Any excuse for a party, eh, girls? The trick will be keeping the idea hidden from him. He's got such a nosy beak, he's bound to cotton on to what we're up to."

Gemma leaned in and said quietly, "Maybe he'll go away for a break in the spring. He did mention that he was hoping to go down to Cornwall to see an old aunt down there, take his mum with him."

The idea sparked Ruth's brain into action. "That's not too far away. Let's try and discreetly persuade him and then action something between us then. Oops, he's coming back. Act naturally."

Hilary tipped her head back and roared with laughter, startling Ruth.

"What's so funny?" Steven asked, whisking his glass off the bar and sipping at his G&T.

"That Ruth, she is a one. The things she comes out with at times, has me in stitches."

Ruth smiled awkwardly, hoping against hope that Steven wouldn't ask her to reveal what she'd said that had forced Hils to laugh so hard. Luckily, Denis came back and ordered a pint at the bar for James, distracting Steven.

"That's great news. I'll take it through to him, Denis," Ruth announced quickly.

"Wait, I need to hear what's so funny first," Steven said.

Ruth was halfway across the function room by now and called over her shoulder, "Ask Hils, she'll fill you in." She chuckled, knowing Hilary would be cursing her for the rest of the evening.

She pushed open the door and stopped dead in her tracks. Raised voices could be heard coming from one of the rooms off the hallway. She moved closer and placed her ear to the door. The voice was unmistakably Jilly's. It would appear she wasn't happy about the way the main banqueting hall had been decorated. *Ha, that serves you right, missus. You should have kept your mouth shut about the foyer, and then Steven would have had enough time to have worked his magic in the other areas of the hotel.*

The handle rattled, and the door swiftly opened. Ruth spilt some of James' beer as she toppled slightly.

"You! What are you doing? Eavesdropping?" Jilly's anger distorted her face.

"No. Sorry. I was passing by on my way to take my boyfriend his drink."

"Where is he?"

"He's the replacement drummer in the band. He kindly stepped in at the last minute for *you*."

"For *me*? You make it sound as if he's doing me a personal favour," Jilly snapped.

Ruth ran an agitated hand across her face, trying hard to hold on to her temper after giving the author a mouthful in the foyer earlier.

"Speak up, woman. You had enough to say for yourself when you insulted me before."

Ruth's anger bubbled near the surface. She was determined not to rise to the woman's bait but was struggling. "I'll be on my way. You obviously like the sound of your own voice and clearly aren't the least bit interested in what anyone else has to say."

"Why, you…!"

"Yes?" Ruth enquired, tilting her head to raise her ear in the woman's direction.

"Nothing. You're not worth the time of day. Get out of my way."

She tugged Ruth's free arm, which put her off balance. Most of James' drink ended up decorating the nearby wall.

Jilly didn't stick around to see the consequences of her actions. She was off up the hallway faster than a scrawny greyhound out of the traps.

You'll get what's coming to you eventually, Diva Author!

Ruth finally arrived in the banqueting hall and stood by the door watching the band warm up with a well-known Beatles song. Pride puffed out her chest when she saw James strutting his stuff with the two thin drumsticks in tune with the rest of the band.

"Come over, don't be shy," a member of the band shouted.

She approached the small wooden stage area, suddenly feeling embarrassed that she didn't have a drink for the rest of the group. "Sorry, I brought a drink for my—"

"Gents, I'd like you to meet my fiancée and the local private investigator, Ruth Morgan," James announced.

She cringed inwardly when she heard him say the F-word. It would take her a while before the reality sets in. "Sorry, I had an accident in the hallway and spilled most of it. Do you guys want me to get you a drink?"

"No. We're fine. We've put an order in at the bar. They'll keep us topped up throughout the evening," the man who appeared to be in charge of the band replied. He went on to introduce the other three members: Zac on the base guitar, Drew on the trumpet, and he was Brian, the lead vocalist as well as the expert saxophonist. "We can't thank James enough for standing in at the last minute. He told us he was rusty. Are you aware that he tells big fat lies, Ruth?"

She laughed. "I knew he'd remember all the strokes once he started playing. You were lucky he was here tonight. Professional drummers are hard to come by at short notice, I believe."

"We're incredibly grateful to you both. I hope it doesn't spoil your evening too much, James helping us out like this."

Ruth waved a hand at Brian. "Not at all. He's here in spirit. I think he would much rather be helping you guys out than attending a boring function. Isn't that right, James?"

"Yep. I'm having a blast. I've got news for you, Ruth. The first opportunity I get, I'm going to look out for a second-hand drum kit and set it up in the garage."

Ruth raised an eyebrow. "Oh, you are, are you? We'll have to see about that. Not sure Mrs Sanders will appreciate the noise. We might lose her as a dog sitter."

The band members all laughed. Ruth stepped closer and handed James his drink.

"It was worth a try," he said, accepting it and holding the half-filled glass in the air. "Since when did I start drinking halves?" he jested.

"Okay, I'd better get back to the others. Have fun, guys. Keep him in line, don't take any hassle from him." She messed up James' hair and then bent to kiss his cheek.

"I'll see you later. Thanks for the thought regarding the pint, if nothing else."

The other band members laughed and waved goodbye. They began rehearsing again as she left the room. In the hallway, she found Sian leaning against the wall.

"Hello, Sian, is everything all right?"

A shuddering breath left the woman's body, and her head slowly lowered. "Hello there. I'll survive. How are you?"

"I'm fine. I'm more concerned about you. I have a sympathetic ear if you'd like to test it out?"

"Thanks for the offer. I'm having a small breather before I get on with the next job on my agenda."

"Umm…if you don't mind me saying, didn't Jilly fire you and Megan earlier?"

She smiled weakly as if the effort made her cheeks hurt. "That's usual for her. She fires us at least five or six times a week, especially if things don't go according to plan."

"How do you do it? Put up with her foul moods?"

She shrugged and held her arms out to the sides. "Most of the time I enjoy my job. It can be a thrill seeing to Jilly's every need, although this entire week has been an absolute chore for both me and Megan to contend with. I think there's something going on that neither me nor Megan are aware of. Frankly, I don't know how she expects us to do our jobs when she keeps secrets from us."

"Any idea what type of secret? Sorry, tell me to keep my nose out if you want to."

"Honestly, I'd tell you if I knew. I don't have the foggiest idea."

"Is it personal or to do with her career?" Ruth asked, ever one for burrowing beneath the surface searching for the truth.

"No idea in the slightest. We have to wait until she sees fit to tell us. In the meantime, she expects us to take the brunt of her anger."

Ruth shook her head. "I couldn't do it. Spending ten minutes with her would be enough for me to want to strangle her. She speaks to people like they're dirt. Has she ever said a kind word to you since you started working for her?"

Sian's lips parted and broke into a slight smile. "I think she praised me for a job well done at a book signing event back in two thousand and sixteen. It was a fleeting moment, never to be repeated."

"Shame on her. You can do so much better than work for someone who fails to appreciate you. Do you have any job satisfaction at all? Sorry, don't answer that, I'm being far too inquisitive."

"No, it's fine. Yes, I love my job, the day-to-day organising it takes to sort out her calendar of events throughout the year. Dealing with the media aspect is one of the best jobs around. I really wouldn't change that side of things for all the tea in China."

"Surely you could switch your employer and still manage to do all the things you love, couldn't you?"

"That type of thing rarely happens in our line of business. People tend to stick with their staff for years."

"You mean there is a glut of famous people who treat their

employees in the same way, and the staff put up with the situation, like you do?"

"Yes. The trouble is, the job pays well. I'm on a damn good income and loath to give it up."

"This is all about the money? Are you married?"

Sian nodded. "To the job."

"Oh, come on, my heart bleeds for you. Are you telling me that you don't get a social life of your own?"

"Rarely. I'm on call twenty-four-seven. She won't have it any other way."

"What? You mean she rings you during the night, expecting you to be at her beck and call then?"

"Quite often she'll pound out a few hours on her computer if her muse strikes during the night."

"But why ring you? What do you do, sit there watching her fingers fly across the keyboard?"

"I keep her supplied with drinks and snacks if she needs them."

Ruth covered her cheeks with her hands. "Oh my, you really do go above and beyond."

"If I didn't, she'd fire me for real."

"I'm confused. How do you know when she's serious or when she's simply blowing off steam?"

Sian's mouth twisted from side to side as she contemplated the question. "You know what? I haven't got a clue. She's unpredictable, like an old banger. One day it starts, and the next it refuses to comply with your wishes."

Ruth chuckled. "That's Betty all over. My car."

Sian smiled. "Well, we could hang around here chatting all evening, but I have work to do, making sure the final arrangements are coming along with the food et cetera. Thank you for letting me vent, Ruth."

"You're welcome to bend my ear any time. If I can be of further assistance throughout the evening, be sure to give me a shout. I'd be more than happy to lend a hand. I might be at a loose end later anyway, what with James playing in the band now."

Sian squeezed Ruth's arm. "I can't thank you and your fella enough for getting me out of a hole with that particular dilemma. Let's face it, you could've told me to take a hike after the way Jilly spoke to you earlier this evening."

"It's forgotten about. If you'll take a bit of advice from an outsider, I would seriously consider your options in the future. I bet if you looked in the situations vacant, you'd be surprised by the number of employers seeking your expert skills."

"I'll consider it. Perhaps it'll come down to that old adage 'better the devil you know' in the end."

"Or she-devil," Ruth corrected her.

They laughed and parted ways. When Sian opened the door to another room in the hallway, Jilly bellowed at her, demanding to know where she'd been and called her a lazy so-and-so. Ruth's anger mounted once more.

Calm down, it's nothing to do with you.

4

*S*he rejoined the rest of the group at the bar. They were all rejoicing and singing Steven's praises as tears of joy ran down his face.

"You daft, emotional bugger." Ruth rubbed his back.

Steven had obviously downed a few G&Ts in her absence because his words were now coming out slurred. "I cwouldn't have done it without you, Ruthy baby." He plastered a slobbery wet kiss on her cheek.

She rolled her eyes at the others. "Do you think we should take our seats?" She was desperate to get Steven settled at the table before he fell over.

"No, there's plenty of time before we have to go through to the main event," Hilary said, downing more of her prosecco, sounding as drunk as Steven.

By now, Ruth was dreading what lay ahead of them. Steven could be a fiery individual with the demon drink inside him from what she could remember. She silently pleaded with Gemma and Lynn to come down on her side.

Eventually, Lynn instructed her husband, Warren, to help her guide Steven through to the banqueting suite. Ruth let out a relieved sigh and ordered a dry white wine from the bar before she followed the others through the hallway and into the large room.

As soon as they entered, Steven shouted without a care in the world, "Look at the state of this place. No comparison to what Ruth and I constwucted, is it? Go on, you have to admit it."

"Not a patch on your masterpiece, Steven, we all accept that," Denis replied, acting as spokesperson for the whole group, instead of Ruth.

They located a large table to accommodate them all on the other side of the room to the band. James waved to them all and then continued to strut his stuff during the warm-up.

"I didn't realise James was so hot on the drums. Maybe he's missed his vocation, Ruth. Perhaps he could go on tour around the world if the right band came calling," Gemma shouted in her ear.

"You think? Hey, I'm not stopping him. He's getting nowhere fast being a copper with that Inspector Littlejohn pushing him back all the time. Maybe I should have a word with him. I'd back him all the way, if that's what he wanted to do. He is pretty amazing, isn't he?"

"A hidden talent for sure," Denis called over the table. "He should capitalise on it before he gets much older. You two could become jet-setting rock stars."

Ruth cringed at the label. "Not sure either of us would relish that tag at our ages. Filling in with a local band for an evening is a bit different to travelling the world with a rock band. I can imagine that would be torturous, playing in a different city every few nights, living out of a suitcase. Nah, definitely not for me."

Denis nodded. "You wouldn't stand in James' way, though, would you? Not if that's where his heart was leading him."

Ruth contemplated Denis's words. *Would I? Stand in his way, if that's what his heart truly desired?* She stared across the room at her intended. He seemed lost in a world of his own. She hadn't seen him this happy in a long time. Maybe there was something in Denis's observation, after all.

Newly engaged, although there was no ring to prove that yet. But could she possibly be about to lose him? If that were to happen, how would she truly cope with that?

As more and more of the residents poured into the banqueting hall, along with a lot of other people Ruth didn't recognise, word soon got around that the weather had turned nasty outside and it had now begun to snow.

"Great, just what we need. I hope everyone who is supposed to turn up arrives, otherwise I'd hate to be in either Sian's or Megan's shoes when Jilly gets wind of it," Ruth whispered in Gemma's ear.

"You worry too much. Just relax and have fun for a change. You're like a coiled spring."

Ruth smiled and shook out the tension in her arms. That was her, a born worrier. She spotted a friend walk into the banqueting hall and excused herself.

"Hello, Louise, are you here on official business this evening?"

"Sort of. Have you met my boss at the paper? Ruth Morgan, the local PI, and this is my boss, Mike Jones."

"Ah, I've heard your name mentioned once or twice around the office. It's a pleasure to meet you, Ruth. Where is she? Have you seen her yet?" He extended his hand for her to shake while his gaze flitted around the room.

Ruth shook his hand. "Pleased to meet you, Mike. Yes, I've met her all right."

He sharply turned to look at her. "I'm not liking your tone. Care to enlighten us?"

"You know how female pop stars are often called divas? Well, let's just say Ms. Bramley takes it to a whole new level. So far, she's given everyone hell tonight, and it's only just turned eight o'clock. Lord knows what lies ahead of us."

"That'll be nerves. I'm sure a grand occasion such as this would tie any one of us in knots and make us antsy, wouldn't it?"

Ruth glanced at Louise and raised an eyebrow as if to say, 'is he for real?'

Louise rolled her eyes. "Mike is a huge admirer of Jilly Bramley's. He has all her books." She motioned to the carrier bag in Mike's hand.

Mike vehemently nodded. "Massive fan, I am. There isn't a better author around than her."

"I've read most of her books. I'm a huge fan also—of her work, not of her as a person after what I've seen in the last few days. What did you think of the hotel lobby?"

Louise smiled. "It was wonderful, very artistic. No, don't tell me you had something to do with that?"

"I did. Steven, the set designer at the Am-Dram club, was mainly responsible for it, but he called on me at the final hour when Jilly ordered him to replace the design he'd already created."

Louise gasped. "Really? Why? What was wrong with it?"

"Absolutely nothing. It was a silver and teal-blue theme. It looked magical, but Jilly pulled a strop and said she detested it. How she expected Steven to strip it down and erect another set within forty-eight hours, I'll never know. But we did it. I offered to lend him a hand. The poor man was so stressed out I thought he was on the verge of having a mental breakdown."

"She loves *The Wizard of Oz* theme, though, right?"

Ruth sighed and shook her head. "Nope, she loathes it. Pulled a right hissy fit earlier on this evening. I stepped forward and told her a few home truths. Her reaction was totally over the top. The people around her, her publicist and her agent, took the brunt of her anger and were sacked on the spot. Oh, they didn't go. I've since spoken to Sian, the publicist, and she assured me that being sacked is a regular occurrence and that she and Megan tend to ignore Jilly when she's in one of her foul moods. What a way to live, right?"

"I won't have you speaking about her like that," Mike snapped. "If the woman has standards that she expects others to work to, then no one should stand in her way of achieving those standards. We all need to understand that some people in this life won't accept anything but the best from those around them. She's a perfectionist in her job; that probably spills over into what she expects from her employees."

Ruth stared at Louise and twisted her mouth. It was obvious the man had a crush on Jilly and wasn't prepared to listen to a bad word against her. "We'll agree to disagree on that one, Mike. You weren't here. The way she spoke to the people she employs was disgusting. It's extremely hard to gauge when you hear things like this second-hand."

"I know vindictive idle gossip when I hear it. Louise, what would you like to drink?"

"Um…I'll have a prosecco, thanks, Mike."

Her boss stomped off without saying another word. "Wow, sounds like he really has it bad for her. I didn't mean to come across as bitchy. All I was doing was explaining what had gone on over the past few days. I'm tired and feeling insensitive because I hate the way the woman treated Steven. I guess I'm guilty of taking his side in this matter. I really didn't mean to cause your boss any offence."

Louise dismissed the notion with a flick of her wrist. "Ignore him. Like I said, he's a super fan of hers, therefore totally biased, in my opinion. She sounds like an overbearing, vile woman to me. Wait, I've just seen something." She pointed over at the band. "Isn't that your James playing the drums?"

"It is. I suppose I forced him into the situation. The original drummer was rushed away in an ambulance. James has always been keen on drumming in the past. I volunteered him for the role. I was trying to make up for Jilly's disappointment a little, not that she appreciated it."

"I never knew his talents extended to that. He seems to be enjoying himself."

"He is. I don't think he's hit a bum note yet." She swept her hand around the room. "Everyone appears to be enjoying the music anyway. That's always a good sign. Do you want to join us?"

"Maybe we'll sit close by, would you mind?"

"Not at all. There's a spare table available next to ours. Let's grab it quick before the masses arrive."

"We're expecting a few other members of our team. Mike insisted that the guys show their support. I think a few other journalists are due as well, some boys from some of the tabloid press. Let's hope Jilly doesn't have another one of her temper tantrums when they show up. If she does, she'll be gutted by the negative press she receives."

"Good point. I heard on the grapevine that she's up for some kind of award. Maybe that will be presented to her tonight."

Louise dipped her head towards her and whispered, "For the bitchiest author perhaps?"

They both roared with laughter which died suddenly when Mike reappeared carrying a pint and a champagne flute. "Something funny you ladies would like to share?"

"Not really. Ruth was telling me how uncomfortable she felt in her dress," Louise filled in quickly.

Ruth suspected she was used to supplying an alternative answer when her boss caught her out. "Yes, I had the unenviable task of deciding whether to wear a thong or my Bridget Jones knickers."

Mike gasped, his cheeks turning red. "Oh my, please, spare me the details. I'd rather not know what you decided on in the end." Then he spun on his heels.

Louise and Ruth laughed as they followed him across the room to the spare table.

"Oh wait, while I'm up I might as well nip to the loo." She winked at Louise and added mischievously, "Might as well see if my Bridget Jones knickers are still in place." She walked away and sniggered when Mike tutted behind her.

Out in the hallway, she located the ladies' toilet and entered one of the cubicles. She heard a dress rustling in the next cubicle and what sounded like someone crying. After spending a penny, she flushed the loo and left the cubicle. The room was empty. She deliberately lingered, slowly washing her hands and drying them under the efficient drier. Still the person didn't appear. Then she opened the door to the entrance of the toilet and closed it. Remaining in the room, she crept back to the sink and waited. The toilet flushed, and the lock on the door slid back. Megan Drake emerged.

"Oh my goodness! You look terrible, Megan. Sorry if that's not what you wanted to hear. Whatever is the matter?"

She appeared startled and tried to step back into the cubicle, but Ruth walked towards her and encouraged Megan to join her.

"Please, if you don't want to tell me what's wrong, that's fine by me. I'm worried about you."

The woman in her late forties sniffled and withdrew a tissue from her sleeve. "I'm being silly. Ignore me. Go back to the party and enjoy yourself. I'll be all right in here. I'll be out in a moment or two."

"I'm not the type to turn my back on someone when they're obviously in distress. Please, won't you confide in me, what's wrong? Maybe I can help in some small way."

"I doubt it. I'm guilty of feeling sorry for myself, that's all. There's not a lot anyone can do about that but me. A good cry was all that was needed. I'll be all right in a moment, I'm sure."

Ruth rubbed the top of Megan's arm. "I sense this is to do with Jilly and her vicious tongue again. Correct me if I'm wrong…"

"You're a very astute lady, Ruth. I'm at my wits' end with her. She's such a needy person, and when people don't or can't deliver, she goes for the jugular. I guess my jugular is feeling pretty raw right now."

"I'm so sorry you've been subjected to a tongue-lashing from her. If it's any consolation, I believe Sian is feeling the same way. I caught her beside herself in the hallway a little while ago."

"You did? Oh my, it's a terrible situation to find ourselves in. None of my other clients disrespect me the way Jilly does."

Ruth chewed on her lip. "Why? Why do you put up with her unreasonable demands in that case?"

Megan shrugged. "Deep down, I know there's a decent person in there trying to emerge. I know she's high-maintenance at times, but when you really get to know the true Jilly Bramley, she's a terrific lady."

"Then why does she behave as if she's the bitchiest woman to ever walk this planet?"

"Only she can answer that, and to be honest with you, I doubt she'd be able to answer it truthfully. She's treated me and Sian the same way for years now. Maybe it's become a habit because she knows we react to her anger."

"Gosh, what an abhorrent and ugly way to treat people. She needs a kick up the backside. I'll willingly have a word with her, if you give me the green light. I detest bullies at the best of times."

"That's very sweet of you to want to become involved, but I doubt it will make a difference. If anything, she's liable to retaliate and treat us even worse than she does already. It would be better if we all agreed to what she wants. It will make for a peaceful life for all of us."

"No one should be expected to live their lives on tenterhooks, waiting for her to explode at the slightest thing that upsets her. You owe it to yourself to seek a better employer. Look at you!"

Megan studied herself in the mirror and then wiped the smudged mascara from under her eyes. "I know you're right. Every evening I tell myself that I don't need to put up with this crap…oh, I don't know, it's as if it's addictive, her treating me this way. Does that even make sense?"

"Not to me. I would never in a million years put up with half the things you and Sian put up with. Is she married?"

"No. Recently divorced. Lincoln was, sorry, *is* such a nice man. He couldn't take her vicious tongue in the end. Their divorce was finalised in September of last year."

"I see. Has her temper improved or worsened since then?"

"It's definitely got worse. I suppose Sian and I are both guilty of feeling sorry for her. Maybe that's why we put up with her arrogance and disrespect."

"That's unbelievable. I don't understand her logic. Surely, you'd think she would treat you guys better knowing the consequences. Isn't that why her marriage failed? Because of her ungrateful attitude?"

Megan nodded. "You're right, I know you are. However, there's knowing it and trying to figure out a way of showing her the errors of her ways without getting a backlash."

"There's no doubting that you and Sian find yourselves in a catch-22 situation, but consider this: the more you're accepting of her angry ways, the more she'll resist the change. What about if you both stood up to her at the same time? You'd be a combined force in your quest for a better working environment, yes?"

"I agree, you're talking sense, but you don't know her like we do. She knows things about us that could harm us if we retaliate."

Ruth inclined her head. "Seriously? Are you telling me that she has some kind of hold over both of you? Is she blackmailing you in some way?"

Megan's eyes widened, as if she'd realised she'd said too much. "I'm sorry, my mouth has a tendency to run away from me at times. Ignore me, I'm talking nonsense."

Ruth was desperate to hear more, but it was obvious Megan wasn't prepared to open up to her further. "Why don't I give you my card? It sounds to me as if you're in a sticky situation, caught between the Devil and the deep blue sea. If I can be of assistance, or if you feel the need to bare your soul in the future, give me a ring." She opened her clutch purse and withdrew a card.

"Thank you. I don't think I'll be needing it. I must go. Please, ignore what I have said during this conversation. A lot of it was just me venting. I feel better now things are out in the open, thank you."

Ruth smiled. "You're welcome. I tend to live by that old adage 'a problem shared is a problem halved'. It's surprising what a difference it can make for someone to air their problems openly. I hope tonight's event is a success and that once the drink starts to flow, Jilly finally relaxes and finds it in her heart to appreciate the efforts of those surrounding her."

Megan held her crossed fingers up and strode towards the door. "You're an exceptional listener, Ruth. Thank you. Enjoy the rest of your evening. If you'd like one, I'm sure I could get you a signed copy of Jilly's latest thriller."

"I'd love one. I know she has her bad side, but it doesn't alter the fact that she's an exceptional author who knows how to spin a gripping tale."

"She does that. Do you know she's about to pass a pivotal mile-stone in her career?"

"Is she? What's that?" Ruth asked, following Megan out of the toilet.

"In about a week's time, if *Shot in the Back* is a raving success, as it's anticipated to be, she should pass the ten million books sold worldwide."

"Wow! What a stunning achievement. She seriously needs to get a life, lighten up and live a little instead of living on her nerves all the time."

Megan chuckled. "I'll pass that message on. On second thoughts, I don't think I will. Thanks for the chat."

"You're welcome," Ruth called out over her shoulder before entering the banqueting hall.

Her eye was drawn to the head table. Jilly was seated there with a young couple. Ruth recognised the girl from a recent magazine article as being her daughter. Maybe the young man was Jilly's son and they were both here to support her. She made a mental note to Google the family later, just because her interest was piqued and she wanted to get to know more about Jilly's family and what made her tick.

Ruth took her seat at the table with her friends, and together they people-watched for the next half an hour or so. Louise and her boss were joined by other members of the press. Ruth tapped Louise on the shoulder a few times to enquire who the men were and was surprised to learn that some of the press had driven up from London to attend the event, even in this ghastly weather. Maybe Jilly was worth all the attention after all, and perhaps Ruth had misjudged how well liked the author was on the circuit.

One of the reporters stepped up to the mic, acting as the master of ceremonies for the evening. He was a tall, lean man with salt-and-pepper highlights running through his short hair, not too unpleasant to look at either. He introduced himself as Barney Roberts.

"It's a privilege and honour for Jilly to have chosen me to be the host at this auspicious occasion. Jilly and I have been friends for years." He turned to face her and smiled. "Dare I tell them how many years?"

Jilly smiled and shrugged. "If you want to."

"Well over twenty years, in fact. And yes, I'm a devoted fan to boot. I love the way she spins a good yarn. An excellent storyteller through and through. One of the finest in her field, I'd say."

Ruth glanced over at Jilly, whose cheeks reddened after the praise was bestowed upon her.

Barney Roberts appeared to revel in the embarrassment he'd caused the author. "Anyway, we're here to celebrate the fact that Jilly has released her nineteenth novel."

The audience erupted, clapping and cheering, even to the point in some cases of giving Jilly a standing ovation.

She smiled at the crowd and then at her daughter and the other young man sitting at the table. They both returned the smile and applauded her.

"As if that news wasn't enough to celebrate, I've been asked by the prestigious Authors Guild to present this fabulous award for services rendered. Jilly, if you wouldn't mind joining me?"

Jilly seemed genuinely surprised by what was taking place. Her daughter urged her to stand. Jilly got to her feet and walked the short distance to where Barney was standing at the mic. They hugged, and he kissed her lightly on both cheeks. They turned sideways so that both of them had access to the mic.

"Thank you, Barney. To say I'm surprised would be a gross understatement. I know you and the others here tonight won't believe me when I say this, but it's totally true, I assure you: I have never regarded writing as a job. Yes, I'm guilty of working long hours to perfect my skills, and that can cause me to become a little touchy at times. I owe Sian and Megan a dozen apologies for constantly taking my foul mood out on them over the years. But when you hit on the right formula, writing comes from your very soul—actually, from three main areas of your body: the soul, the heart and the brain. Without the ability to conjure up likeable characters and write a believable plot, we have nothing."

"It shows, too. Whenever I pick up one of your books, it draws me in. I get lost between the pages, wrapped up in the adventures of your main characters as they hunt down the criminals and enforce justice. It takes a master of their art to have that ability to entertain the audience the way you do on a regular basis. You're to be admired, churning out bestseller after bestseller. I'm sure I'm not alone in wondering how you manage to do it, Jilly. Would you care to share any tips or secrets with any possible budding authors in this audience?"

"That's a tough one. This old bird has been at this writing lark for over twenty-five years. Yes, it gets harder coming up with an original plotline, but once you have the basic idea in place then you need to run with it. Get the first draft down on paper first, that's often the hardest part. The book can be fleshed out during the second or third draft. And yes, take my word for it. By the time the book hits the shelves, you'll *hate* it, having read the darn thing over and over around a dozen times to perfect it."

The audience roared at her openness.

"Are there any budding authors among us?" Barney asked.

Ruth scanned the room and was surprised to see Mike's hand raised. Ruth and Louise stared at each other in surprise.

"I work on the local newspaper—actually, I own it," Mike said. "I'm a huge admirer of your work, Ms. Bramley, and wondered if it's possible to make the transition from journalist to fiction author."

Jilly nodded, acknowledging his question. "I've heard it's possible, but it's a totally new learning curve for the journalist to get their head around. It's one thing telling the news as it happens. It's a different concept entirely creating a believable plot and a likeable bunch of characters who you want the general public to root for."

"Ah, I wondered if that might be the case. I know a few journalists who have tried and failed in the past. I have a few copies of your books with me tonight. Would it be possible for you to sign them for me? Sorry if you think I'm overstepping the mark and being cheeky."

"Not at all. Come and see me afterwards, it would be my pleasure."

Ruth sat back in her chair, amazed at the transformation in the author. Maybe she was devoted to her work and took pleasure in speaking about it openly with her audience of admirers. Perhaps all the nonsense of the past few days was merely down to her wanting to get things right for the people who adored her. *Did she really think that if the hotel looked shabby it would be a bad reflection on her? Not that Steven's artistic flair could ever be classed as being shabby, not in my book.*

Mystified, she watched the author's interaction with a few other members of the crowd who had it in their minds to become authors. She was giving with her advice; not once did she fail or object to answering what was being asked of her.

Eventually, Barney took over the mic again. Jilly started to walk away from him, but he tugged on her arm and reached behind him for the trophy. He presented it, along with a kiss on either cheek once more. Again, Jilly thanked him and went to leave the mic, and he pulled her back. Puzzled, she placed the trophy on the table behind her as he bent down and lifted the cloth on the table closest to him.

"You thought that was the only award coming your way this evening. It isn't. I'm thrilled to announce that this week, sooner than anticipated, with the success of *Shot in the Back,* your worldwide sales have rocketed past the ten million copies sold mark."

Jilly gasped loudly, and tears dripped onto her cheeks, again surprising Ruth. She didn't think the woman had it in her to feel such emotions as pride and gratitude.

"Oh my! I truly wasn't expecting this as you can probably tell by the tears. I'm overwhelmed to have reached this phenomenal achieve-ment. Yes, I know the likes of James Patterson probably has those kinds of figures in a year, but seriously, this achievement couldn't have come about if it wasn't for Sian, my wonderful publicist, and Megan, my talented agent. Thank you, ladies."

Sian and Megan, who were sitting at the head table alongside Jilly and her family, both smiled and nodded, appreciating her singling them out for praise.

Jilly took the plaque and the trophy back to her table, and the band struck up again, encouraging the crowd to take to the floor.

Mike rifled under the table and emerged with a few of Jilly's books. He left his seat and walked over to her, but was sent packing without Jilly adding her autograph. The man appeared devastated, the colour rising in his cheeks proving how embarrassed he was.

So it was all show! You heartless, evil and twisted woman. How could you treat one of your fans like that?

Ruth clawed across the space between the tables and latched on to

Louise's arm. "Poor Mike. Tell him to keep his chin up. If he wants, I'll have a word with Jilly later. I'll get him her autograph."

"Would you? That would be fantastic, Ruth. She's such a beep beep!"

Ruth chuckled. "And some. What a nightmare woman, and there was me thinking I'd done her an injustice by condemning her actions earlier, putting it down to the stress of the evening. Her display of being a pleasant character was all for show. She should be on the stage instead of writing novels for a living. Ugh, I didn't realise how easy it would be to go off people. I hate what she stands for."

"I'm with you on that one. *She* asked him to seek her out, for goodness' sake. What a warped individual she is."

A few minutes later, the hotel staff brought through large platters of food and set up the buffet. Once the go-ahead was given, the crowd queued up. Ruth glanced over at Jilly, who was observing the crowd through narrowed eyes, as if she begrudged them dipping into the food she'd generously laid on.

Wow! She really is a nasty piece of work.

Ruth and her fellow Am-Dram members were the last ones to leave their seats and descend on the buffet. Their plates filled to capacity with vol-au-vents and small triangle sandwiches filled with a mixture of salmon and egg mayonnaise, they returned to their seats. After munching through half the contents on her plate, Ruth pushed the food aside. The sandwiches were dry, and the pastry had soggy bottoms— totally unacceptable to a food connoisseur such as herself. She wouldn't have been seen dead laying on such a poor display at any of her parties. She noted that none of the people seated at Jilly's table ventured over to collect any of the buffet. *Why? Had they already eaten in the hotel's dining room earlier? Or are they intending to eat later, after the event has finished?* Either way, Ruth thought it was a telling sign and one that didn't sit comfortably with her. What a nasty character Jilly Bramley was.

Deciding to ignore the ghastly woman for the rest of the evening, Ruth encouraged Gemma to get on her feet and dance with her.

Gemma was a little tiddly, and as they jived, the fast pace that Ruth spun her had a devastating effect on her balance.

"Oh no, Ruth, stop, I'm going to be sick."

Ruth rushed her out of the room and down the hallway to the ladies' where she listened to Gemma empty her stomach down the toilet.

Not long after, Sian entered the room. "Hello there. Is everything all right with your friend?"

"She's fine. I think I'm guilty of being excessive with my jive moves. She's in there now, regurgitating the buffet. I'm surprised your table didn't have any food. May I ask why?"

"Jilly wants to show her appreciation later on this evening and has ordered room service to be set up in her suite."

"Ah, I thought it might be something along those lines."

"Was the buffet okay?" Sian asked, touching up her lipstick in the mirror.

Ruth took the comb out of her clutch bag and ran it through her hair, yelping a little when it caught on a knot at the end. "It was fine. I didn't eat much because once it was sitting in front of me, I went off it."

"Looks like the others enjoyed it. Some of them are even going up for seconds."

"There was a lot left. Let's hope there isn't too much waste. Can't see Jilly liking that if there is."

"She's fine. I think after all the stress of earlier, winning the awards has definitely lightened her mood. I'd better get back now, before they send out a search party for me."

"One last question before you leave. May I ask who is the young man sitting at the table with you? I thought it might be Jilly's son."

"No. She doesn't have a son. Fiona is an only child. Jake is Fiona's boyfriend. They've been together for the past year or so now. Nice chap, he is."

"Thanks for that. Sorry for being a nosy beak; it's hard to switch off sometimes. I want to know the ins and outs of a duck's backside."

The cubicle door opened, and Gemma came out, looking green

around the gills. "Oh God, my tongue feels like sandpaper. I don't think I'm going to be able to stay here much longer, Ruth, I'm sorry."

Ruth placed an arm around her shoulder. "No problem, I'll have to ring for a taxi to take you home."

"Would you? Oh gosh, I think I'm going to be sick again." Gemma ran into the toilet and slammed the door.

Sian cringed, waved Ruth farewell and escaped the room before Gemma emptied her stomach for the second time. Ruth stepped out into the hallway and fished her phone out of her bag. She called the local taxi firm and managed to book one to pick Gemma up in fifteen minutes. Not long after she ended the call, shouting came from one of the rooms further down the hallway. Looking around her, she eased down the carpeted hall and came to a standstill outside one of the rooms. The shouting appeared to have died down. She placed her ear against the door but heard nothing. Shrugging, she turned around and went back to see how Gemma was doing, her mind still wandering back to the incident.

"Oh, Gemma. You do look rough. The taxi should be here soon. Why don't we wait outside? I know it'll be cold, but at least you'll get some fresh air in your lungs."

"What about the others? They'll think I'm rude if I disappear without saying goodbye."

"No, they won't. Don't be so silly. Come on, I'll nip back and grab your bag and coat and make your excuses. You wait in the hallway for me."

"Maybe I should stay in here instead."

"All right. I'll be right back." Ruth rushed out of the toilet and swept through the banqueting hall to the rest of the group. "Sorry, guys, Gemma sends her apologies. She's feeling really rough. I've called a taxi to take her home."

"Oh no. Want me to come and help?" Hils asked. She grabbed Gemma's coat and handbag off the seat and handed them to Ruth.

"No. You stay and enjoy yourselves. I'll only be five minutes." She smiled and returned to the ladies' toilet with Gemma's possessions.

Gemma was in the cubicle again. Ruth sighed, anxious about her friend's welfare.

"How are you doing in there?"

"I'm not sure I can move. I have a griping pain in my stomach. Why the heck did I eat so much of that crappy food?"

"Don't. I hope it wasn't the food, otherwise there will be dozens of people in the same situation as you later on this evening. Do you honestly think that if anything was wrong with the food it would have shown up by now?"

"I don't know. I feel so ill, Ruth. I think I'm going to have to go to the hospital."

"Really? Oh my, I'll come with you in that case. I can't let you go alone."

The toilet flushed, and a doubled-over Gemma emerged from the cubicle. Ruth rushed to assist her and guided her to the sink. She ran some cold water on her hand and applied it to the back of Gemma's neck. She had no idea if she was doing the right thing or not, but something in the back of her mind sounded familiar.

Gemma moaned a little. "That feels good. I don't care what my hair looks like. I'll go to the hospital alone, you stay here."

"Are you sure? I don't mind. We can't move until you feel a little better, hon. We daren't. If you puke in the back of the taxi, the driver will throw a wobbly."

"I know. Let's leave it a few minutes. Why can't I stand upright? What do you think is going on?"

"I haven't got a clue. If I didn't know any better, I'd say you had a bout of food poisoning."

"No! That can't be right."

Ruth tried to help her stand, but Gemma only managed to stretch her body thirty percent of its usual capacity. "You really are in a bad way, aren't you? Let's try and get you outside."

They gingerly made their way through the hotel and out of the front door. Ruth draped Gemma's winter coat around her shoulders and placed her against the wall for extra support. Ruth rubbed her arms, trying to get the circulation going against the biting temperature as the snow fell in front of them.

"It always makes you feel colder watching the snow fall, doesn't it? How are you?"

"Rough, plain and simple. I hope the taxi won't be much longer. I'll be fine if you want to get back to the party, Ruth."

"No way. Wait, here we are, there's a taxi pulling up now. I'll help you down the steps to the car."

"It's too dangerous. You'll slip in your sandals. Please, I insist, you stay here."

The taxi driver leaned across his seat and wound down the window. "Come on, love, I haven't got all night."

Furious, Ruth motioned for him to get out of the car. "You're going to have to help us."

The driver shouted an expletive, wound up his window and left the car. He wore a sheepskin coat which was covered in snow by the time he reached them. "This isn't part of the job. I'm only doing this because you've caught me in a good mood this evening."

"Really? Okay, thanks for your help. My friend is desperately ill and needs to be taken to A&E right away."

"Too much alcohol pass your lips this evening, love?"

"Not at all. Please hurry," Ruth growled.

"Oh, Ruth. I don't think I can move from this spot. I'm going to pass out. My head is swaying."

"Oh crap!" The driver groaned beside her.

"It's no good. You're going to have to carry her."

"No way! Not in my job description, love. I'm out of here." He turned and started to walk down the steps.

"You do that, and I'll report you to the council. I'm good at making up stories. I'll get them to revoke your licence. She's ill and needs our help."

He retraced his steps, bent over and hoisted Gemma in a fireman's lift.

She moaned heavily.

"Are you coming as well?" he asked.

"Only to the car."

"Don't bother. I can manage her myself. Ha, some friend you are."

"Shut up, she's needed here. I'll be fine, Ruth, don't listen to him. Go back and enjoy yourself," Gemma shouted.

The driver carefully walked back to the car. Gemma managed to wave from her position slumped over his back while Ruth returned to the party, riddled with guilt for not going with her. The party was still in full swing. The people on her table, although devastated that Gemma had to leave, were still having a blast, knocking back the alcohol and making fools of themselves on the dance floor.

Ruth was in conversation with Steven when Jilly tapped him on the shoulder. "Hello, I'd like a private chat with you if that's possible?"

Steven stuttered a little when he responded, "Of course. Where? Here?"

With no hint of a smile, even though her voice had softened considerably compared to the last time she'd spoken to him, Jilly replied, "There's a room we've been using in the hallway, the one nearest the ladies' toilet. Meet me there in thirty minutes, if you would."

Steven nodded with all the enthusiasm of a child awaiting their first experience of Santa. Jilly swivelled on her heel and joined the rest of her group as they left the room.

Ruth clutched his arm, giving it an excited squeeze. "Wow, maybe she's reconsidered and wants to apologise to you. Crikey, what if she wants to recompense you with payment? That would be amazing, Steven. It would be the cherry on top of the cake. It hasn't been that bad an evening after all. Well, except for what happened to Gemma."

"Now don't go feeling guilty about that. If you'd gone with her you would've probably been stuck in A&E for three or four hours. I'm sure she'll get seen quicker if they're aware she's on her own."

Ruth frowned and chuckled. "Not sure if your logic is accurate on that one, Steven. Anyway, I'm pleased Jilly wants to see you, just wish I could be a fly on the wall during the meeting. Oh, what I wouldn't give for one of my PI spy mics right now. I'd nip into the room and hide it under the desk, then I'd be able to hear what was going on first-hand."

They both roared.

"You are a little minx at times, Ruth. Truthfully, I wish you could be there, too. I still have my doubts about the woman. She seems to blow hot one minute and cold the next. I could do with you by my side for moral support. Not sure I could take another dressing down so soon after the last one she handed out."

She patted his knee. "Now don't go overthinking things and getting yourself in a tizzy. I'll buy you another drink. G&T?"

"All right, you've twisted my arm."

Ruth wandered over to the bar, jigging to the music while she waited to be served. All in all, she'd had a pleasant evening, far better than she could've anticipated after the way it had started out. She missed having James by her side, but she felt comforted knowing he was close to hand and doing a remarkable job with the band.

The barman served her drinks. James appreciated the pint she took him, and then she returned to sit with Steven and the rest of the group. Everyone was excited for Steven and eager to learn what lay ahead of him. Ruth had seen several different sides to the woman this evening, and she couldn't help wondering which Jilly would show up when Steven's meeting came around. She anxiously counted down the minutes, glancing at her watch every few seconds until finally twenty-eight minutes had passed.

"Sorry to interrupt, Steven, it's nearly time." She stood and drew him in for a tight hug. "Take care and knock her dead. Maybe she wants to discuss working with you at another venue in the future."

"What an absolute dream that would be. I'm willing to put the way she spoke to me behind me if she does. Okay, I'm going. See you soon. You guys will be the first to know." He kissed Ruth on the cheek and flounced away, mincing across the floor.

Ruth tried to involve herself in the conversation going on around her but found herself distracted, pondering what was being said between Jilly and Steven. That was until a woman's piercing scream filled the room. Ruth was the first to rush to the woman's aid. "What's wrong?"

One shaking hand covered her mouth while the other pointed into the hallway through the open door. Ruth brushed past the woman, who was an out-of-town stranger, and peered into the hallway. Steven, his legs bent, leaned against the wall, staring ahead of him.

Something was wrong. "Steven? Are you all right?"

The woman shouted something behind her that sounded like 'he's covered in blood'. Hesitantly, she moved towards him. He appeared to be stunned.

She was a few feet away from him now, and that was when she spotted the blood on his hands. Her heart skipped several beats and then mimicked a bass drum, beating hard against her ribs.

The woman behind her screamed again and shouted, "Don't go near him. Please, someone call the police."

Ruth looked back and shouted to a man standing alongside the woman, "Get her back in the room. Leave this to me." She watched the man tug the woman out of sight and then slowly turned back to speak to Steven. "Sweetheart, can you hear me?"

His head inched its way round to face her. "She's…she's…dead, Ruth!"

"What? Who? How? Where?" She fired off the questions as she approached him. "Steven, speak to me."

He shook his head, his eyes panic-stricken, then he glanced down at his hands which were covered in blood. "Ruth, it's her blood."

5

"*W*hose? Not Jilly's?" Ruth gasped. She raced to his side. He inched his way along the wall to get away from her. "Don't touch me. Oh, no…this can't be happening…not again."

"Steven, you're not making sense. What do you mean?"

"Please, Ruth, tell me what to do before the police arrive."

"Just tell them the truth. They'll believe you. Where is she?"

His gaze moved to the open door a few feet away. "In there. I swear, I didn't do it."

"I believe you. Stay there. Let me see for myself."

"No. You mustn't go in there. Let the police deal with it. Crap, what will they do to me? I was in there. Look at me, I'm covered in her blood."

"Why? Why are you covered in her blood, Steven?"

"I tried to help. Felt for a pulse and I slipped. My legs were trembling that much at the sight of her lying there."

"Okay, keep calm. I'll take a look." She stepped into the room. The large lamp on the table created an eerie glow. Her shadow moved across the wall as she neared Jilly's body.

The woman was slouched in the gold velour easy chair close to the desk, a glass of red wine, which had spilled its contents, on the floor beneath her. Ruth moved closer to the woman. A huge patch of blood coated her stomach, and the material on her gold lamé dress was slashed. Ruth gasped and took a step back.

Voices filled the hallway behind her. In the distance, she heard them asking Steven the same questions over and over again, "Why? How did it happen?"

It was obvious to Ruth there was no point attempting to revive the woman—she was stone-cold dead. Everything was a blur for the next five minutes. Her main priority was to ensure the police had been called, then, with the help of the hotel manager and his staff, she shooed everyone back into the banqueting hall while they awaited the police.

Ruth was experienced enough to keep her distance from Steven. She stood within five feet of her friend, close enough to comfort him but far enough away to refrain from getting any blood on her clothes or hands. She'd kicked herself mentally for going into the room to witness the scene for herself, knowing now that she could be seen as a possible accessory if the police saw fit. Damn and blast. All she needed now was her arch rival in the force to show up.

As if her thoughts had summoned the woman up, Inspector Janice Littlejohn marched down the hall towards her. Snapping at her heels was her partner, DS Joe Kenton. Both of them had been omitted from Ruth's Christmas list for years.

"You! Why am I not surprised you're involved?"

Livid, Ruth could already feel her blood heating up her veins. This damn woman never failed to have this kind of effect on her. "*Involved*? You might want to rephrase that and try to uncover the facts before you start slinging accusations around, Inspector."

"You're standing here, aren't you? Therefore, you're involved."

Ruth glared at the woman and shook her head. "You're a real piece of work, you know that?"

"Doing my job and seeing things as I find them, Miss Morgan. If you'll go with the constable, we've arranged to carry out the interviews in one of the hotel rooms. You and your friend here will be first up." Littlejohn's gaze narrowed when it flicked between Ruth and Steven.

"He's in shock. Be gentle with him," she warned, aware that her words would be disregarded immediately by the obstinate inspector.

"What's going on?" James came rushing out of the banqueting room towards them.

"It would appear that the inspector here is going to regard me as a suspect," Ruth declared, shooting from the hip before the inspector had a chance to let him know what was going on.

"You're guilty of twisting my words again, Miss Morgan, not for the first time over the years. All we want to do is interview you. This man, he's a friend of yours?"

Ruth sighed and puffed out her cheeks. This woman was unbeliev-able. She'd been in her current role for over five years now, and as far as Ruth could tell hadn't bothered to get to know any of the inhabitants in Carmel Cove in that time. *Shame on you, Inspector! Everyone is a suspect in your eyes—at least that's how it comes across most of the time.*

"He's Steven Swanson. He works as a caretaker at Highgate School. He's also in charge of the set designs at the local Am-Dram club based at the town hall."

"I'm aware of where it's based, Miss Morgan. Has he told you why he did it?"

"What? You insensitive piece of…"

Littlejohn tilted her head and raised an eyebrow. "Go on!"

"Steven didn't do it. If he had, do you really think he'd hang around waiting for you guys to show up?"

Ruth took a step nearer to Steven and placed a hand on his shoulder.

"Don't touch him," Littlejohn snapped.

"I'm comforting my *innocent* friend."

"I'll be the judge of whether he's innocent or not. Now, back away. Constable, place this man in the room assigned for the interviews. I'll be in shortly." Although she spoke to the male constable behind her, Littlejohn's gaze remained on Ruth.

Feeling uncomfortable, Ruth shuffled her feet.

Littlejohn swiftly cottoned on to her discomfort. "Something bothering you, Miss Morgan?"

"The fact there's a murderer in the hotel doesn't sit well with me, if you must know."

"We'll have the problem sorted soon, you don't have to worry about that."

Ruth chewed on the inside of her mouth. Experience told her not to wind the inspector up, but there was no way she was going to stand back and allow Littlejohn to ride roughshod over Steven. He was innocent—she had to get that point across. The trouble was, that whenever Ruth tried to enforce upon the inspector that she was barking up the wrong tree, the inspector dug her heels in hard and fast. "You're wrong," she muttered.

Littlejohn was taller than Ruth. She leaned forward and placed her face inches from Ruth's. "We'll see about that. It's not often we find a suspect still on-site when we arrive, but now and again a break comes our way that we just can't ignore."

"And you're an idiot if you think Steven is capable of killing her."

"Constable, escort Miss Morgan back to the banqueting room and watch her until I'm ready to question her."

A female constable grabbed Ruth by the elbow and guided her back up the hallway. They passed James. He looked as if he'd had the stuffing knocked out of him. With her eyes she beseeched him for help. He shrugged. Ruth knew as well as he did what an impossible task it would be to try to reason with the inflexible inspector.

6

The banqueting room was a mixture of stunned silence and shocked murmurings. In a daze, Ruth was escorted back to her table by the constable.

"Oh my, Ruth. Are you all right?" Hils asked, rushing to sit beside her.

"I'm all right. Steven isn't."

Denis leaned forward. "Why? What's wrong with him?"

"I think they're going to arrest him."

Everyone around the table gasped.

"They can't do that without a good reason. What proof do they have?" Lynn asked, resting her arm across Ruth's shoulder.

She swept a shaking hand over her face. "He's covered in her blood. He swears blind he didn't do it."

"No!" Hils cried. "Not Steven, he's not capable of killing anyone, although, he was really upset, you know, what with the way she treated him."

Ruth stared at her and shook her head. "No, Hilary, don't even go there. He couldn't do something as heinous as this, not Steven." What she wasn't about to tell them was what he'd said: 'This can't be happening...not again'. *Has he killed before? Or was he saying he'd been caught up in a similar incident in the past?* At the moment, Ruth had far more questions than answers galloping through her mind. She hated being in this situation, stuck out of the way when she would be far more use out there, in the thick of it all. Poor Steven. She was desperate to know how he was getting on, whether the inspector was being gentle with him or treating him badly as if he were a hardened criminal. Ruth knew in her heart of hearts he was innocent, even if his final words to her had left a lingering doubt in her mind.

James re-entered the room and rushed to be with them. "How are you doing?" he asked Ruth, taking Hils' place next to her and wrapping his own comforting arm around her shoulder.

"It's not me I'm worried about. What's going on out there?"

"Littlejohn is going to start interviewing Steven in a second or two."

"It's serious, isn't it?"

"Looks that way, love."

"We need to get him a solicitor, James. He has a right to one before she starts interrogating him. He's in bits, liable to say something that he'll regret later," she rattled off, her mouth trying hard to keep up with the speed of her brain.

"Calm down. You're not going to be any help to him if you go off the rails. He's going to need you more than ever."

Ruth blew out a few breaths and shook the tension out of her arms in a bid to calm herself. "I feel so helpless." She reached for her clutch bag, withdrew her phone and scrolled through her contacts. "Ah, here it is. He's gonna love me for ringing him up this late on a Saturday night."

"Who, Wayne?" James asked.

Ruth nodded and punched in her solicitor friend's number. He answered the call within a few rings.

"Ruth, is that you? Is everything okay?"

"Hi, Wayne. I appreciate how late it is but I'm in dire need of your expert advice."

"Sounds ominous. Don't worry about the time. I'm watching a

rerun of *Mad Max* for want of something better to do. How can I help?"

"I'm desperate and a bit emotional, so forgive me if everything comes out a little jumbled."

"Thanks for the warning. Take a few deep breaths and then spill."

"That's all I've been doing since the incident occurred. Okay, here goes. You know I'm a member of the Am-Dram club."

"Yes, you have been for years."

"Well, some of us, actually most of us..."

"Get to the point, Ruth," he interjected good-naturedly.

"We're at an event at the Carmel Cove Hotel, being staged by the author Jilly Bramley."

"I heard there was something going on over there tonight, it's the main reason I decided to stay in. Well, that and the ghastly weather we're having. Anyway, go on."

"To put it bluntly, there's been a major crime down here, and a friend of mine needs your help."

"Now you've grabbed my attention. What sort of help?"

"He's being interviewed by the police without any form of representation. I need you down here, Wayne."

"What the heck?"

"Will you come down and rescue him?"

"What's the officer in charge interviewing him regarding?"

"The author I mentioned before, well, she's been murdered."

"What?" he shouted, almost deafening her.

"You heard. I know that Steven didn't do it, Wayne. You have to help him."

The TV went off in the background. Her heart lifted; she knew Wayne wouldn't let her down.

"I'll be there in two shakes of a grandfather clock's pendulum."

In spite of the gravity of the situation, she found herself chuckling at his misused analogy. "I get what you meant. Thanks so much, Wayne. I really appreciate it. I'll see you soon then."

"I know you wouldn't ring me if it wasn't important. I'll see you soon, say, five to eight minutes?"

"Excellent. I'll try and dissuade the inspector from interviewing him before you get here. Although I fear I'll have my work cut out for me."

"Do you want me to have a word over the phone?"

"Would you? Hang on, I'll have to leave the room. Damn, I can't, they have me under some form of house arrest."

"What? They can't do that."

"Okay, maybe that was me extending the truth a little. Let me try and get past my babysitter."

James shook his head. "Bypass me, why don't you?"

"What do you mean?" Ruth asked, her brow furrowing.

James grabbed the phone and left the room. Ruth watched him and remained in the same position, her mouth hanging, her numerous fillings on show, until he returned. He placed the phone in her hand and said, "Sorted. I do have my uses after all."

"Sorry, I didn't mean to discount you. If anything, I was trying my hardest not to get you involved, so you didn't get into bother with Littlejohn."

"I know. I couldn't sit back and do nothing. Steven is a good man. He deserves to be treated like a human being and not someone who is always in trouble with the police. Littlejohn wasn't happy, but she's accepted that she possibly overstepped the mark in her eagerness to capture a killer."

"She's such an idiot at times. How on earth she hasn't got the sack, well, it's beyond me."

He winked at her. "I'd say it's only a matter of time before that happens, especially when the grapevine at work starts to spread a rumour about what happened this evening."

Shocked, Ruth leaned in and whispered, "Seriously, you'd do that for me?"

"I'd do anything for you, the same as I have done in the past, if you'll let me."

She held his face in her hands and kissed him.

"Excuse us, you two. Maybe you should get a room while we're here," Hils chastised them jokingly.

Ruth's cheeks heated up. "Sorry, folks. I'm not sure who's more embarrassed, between you and me."

The group laughed, but their laughter faded when a scream came from the hallway. Seconds later, the constable who had shown Ruth to her table was helping Fiona, Jilly's daughter, to her seat at the top table. Her boyfriend was supporting her on the other side. They both appeared to be shell-shocked.

"I wonder where Sian and Megan are," Ruth uttered under her breath.

"Not sure. Those attending the party all left the room at least half an hour before Jilly's body was discovered," James replied.

"Well, Steven only went to meet Jilly because she requested it. We're all witnesses to that fact, aren't we?"

"You're right. Thinking logically about it, Steven was hardly likely to do anything to Jilly, knowing that all of us were aware they had a meeting planned."

"Maybe Littlejohn should be told about that."

"Want me to try?" James suggested.

Ruth shook her head. "No, leave things as they stand at the moment. Wayne can wipe the floor with her when he turns up."

"I'd love to be around when he does that," James said.

"Go. You have every right to be out there. It's me Littlejohn has a grudge with, not you."

He shook his head. "I'd rather not push the boundaries just yet. I'm not exactly high up on her list of people to trust after her complaint about me ended up in a warning."

Ruth's mouth turned down at the sides. "Sorry, that was my fault."

"Nonsense. You solved the crime before she even started to get going on it. Sour grapes and searching for comeuppance was what drove her to tell tales about me. I'm over it."

"You're a good man, James Winchester." She grasped his hand and then looked over at Jilly's daughter. She was inconsolable, which was to be expected if she'd just been told about her mother's death. *Where were Sian and Megan? Could they be guilty of murdering their boss? Maybe they collaborated to do away with her.*

Just then the door opened again, and in walked the two ladies in question. They supported each other as they made their way over to the table to join Jilly's daughter and her boyfriend. The three women hugged and broke down in tears. It was a heartbreaking display of raw emotion. Anyone observing the scene would have to have a heart made of stone not to be affected by it.

Ruth wiped away a tear that had fallen onto her cheek. "What a dreadful situation to be in, for all of them."

"They'll get through it, eventually. I wonder where they all were," James replied, taking a sip from his beer.

"I was wondering the same thing. Were they together? Do they have alibis?"

James chortled. "Ever the PI. It does seem strange that there was no one with Jilly. That has to be an anomaly in itself, right?"

"Well, I've never seen Jilly alone. There's always been someone with her. She came across as the needy type to me. Of course, if her intention was to apologise to Steven for treating him badly, maybe she dismissed the others to save face. Pure conjecture on my part, of course."

"A realistic viewpoint," James agreed. "So where were the others?"

"I don't know. That's something I intend to find out. If Littlejohn thinks I'm going to back off, she's got another think coming."

She'd done it again, summoned up the she-devil while talking about her. Standing in the doorway was Littlejohn, beckoning her with her forefinger, a stern expression on her dark-skinned face.

"Oh no, you've been summoned. Good luck," James said as Ruth left her seat.

"Thanks. By the angry look on her face, I'm going to need it."

Her legs were shaking as she made her way towards her nemesis. She refused to let the woman know how much anxiety was trickling through her veins, so she plastered on a smile. The inspector turned, without saying a word, expecting her to follow.

Once she and the inspector were alone in the designated room, Ruth let out an involuntary shudder.

"Are you cold, Miss Morgan?" The inspector narrowed her eyes and smirked.

"In case you hadn't noticed, it's snowing outside, which tends to make the temperature drop. As you can see, I'm hardly dressed to combat the cold." She stroked an imaginary strike in the air. *One to me!*

"Indeed. Take a seat. There's no need to be nervous. All I want to do is have an informal chat."

"Do I need a solicitor?"

"I don't know, do you?" the inspector shot back without a pause.

Ruth shook her head. "No. How's Steven? I'd like to see him as soon as I can."

"He's with his solicitor. I thought I'd leave them to talk for a while and come and question you instead." She withdrew her notebook and pen from her pocket, her usual sidekick nowhere to be seen, hence her having to take her own notes. "Now, perhaps you'd care to tell me what your part in all this is?"

Ruth scratched her head and frowned. "Not sure I'm liking the inference. Care to tell me what you're referring to?"

Littlejohn's eyes blazed, but the faintest smile tugged at her lips. *Maybe she has wind. I doubt if that's a smile intended for me.*

"This evening. This event. What's your part in it? Why are you here this evening? Is that clear enough?"

"Oh, right. Yes. I was invited along with the other Am-Dram club members." Ruth had learned over the years only to give the inspector the simplest of answers. She had no intention of divulging too much. Why make the inspector's job easier than it should be? It wasn't like she owed the woman anything after the callous way she'd treated Ruth over the years.

"Any specific reason why you received the invite?"

"Because we're well thought of in the community, I should imagine. Didn't you receive one?"

Littlejohn's eyes formed tiny slits. "No, I guess the invitation got lost in the post."

"That's a shame. It's been a fantastic evening, right up until…"

"Until the guest of honour's death?"

"Yes, that was unfortunate."

Littlejohn's eyes widened, and she tilted her head. "Just like your phrasing, I'd say. I'd hardly call someone getting murdered an unfortunate incident."

"Granted. Poor choice of words."

"So, perhaps you can tell me what Steven Swanson's role was here this evening?"

"He created the set in the foyer. Impressive, right?"

The inspector shrugged her slender shoulders.

"Did the victim, Jilly Bramley, appreciate his efforts?"

You know she didn't. I'm not stupid, I know where this is leading.

"Yes, in the end she did."

The inspector's expertly sculpted eyebrow shot up. "Not in the beginning?"

"No, as I'm in no doubt you're fully aware."

"I sense a reluctance in you, Miss Morgan. Don't you want to help your friend?"

"Of course I do. I'm also aware of how you personally like to take any information given and bend the truth, shall we say?"

"Hardly. The facts have been clearly laid out for me by the hotel manager. All I'm trying to do is ascertain the facts from those concerned. Are you saying you're unwilling to cooperate? Because if you are, all you'll be doing is raising my suspicions."

Ruth shrugged and let out a large sigh. "So what's new? You tend to be suspicious of me most of the time anyway."

"I don't know how you work that out, Miss Morgan. Over the past few years your tenaciousness has become tedious, I'll grant you that; however, putting my opinion aside, I have to admit that you do get results."

Ruth placed a hand over her heart. "Gosh, are you paying me a compliment?"

The inspector shrugged then changed the subject, as if she'd revealed something she wasn't entirely comfortable with. "The hotel manager also told me that you helped Steven create the display in the foyer. Did you?"

"I can't deny it. My input was far less than Steven's, though. He came up with the idea and instructed me on how he wanted the display to look."

"Am I right in thinking Jilly Bramley wasn't happy with the results?"

"That's right."

The inspector seemed surprised by the admission. "Wasn't there, how shall I say this? A little contretemps between you all earlier this evening?"

Ruth's gaze remained fixed on the inspector, aware that she would be looking for any signs of her displaying any form of discomfort. "I wouldn't go as far as to say that. Clearly Jilly wasn't altogether happy with how the display turned out. She's been a little demanding, over the past few days."

"In what respect?" The inspector fidgeted in her chair and sat forward.

"In that Steven had already created a beautiful display in the foyer this week. However, when Jilly saw it, she tore it to pieces, figuratively speaking. Steven rang me out of desperation to help him out. Together, over the past few days, we've busted a gut to rip down the old set and erect the new one."

"I see, and Jilly Bramley still wasn't happy with the results?"

"Not really, no. But it was too late to alter things a second time. I'm not dumb, I realise where this is all leading, and I have to tell you, you're wrong. Neither Steven nor I have it in us to kill someone, whether they've royally ticked us off or not," she stated passionately.

The inspector tilted her head again. "I wasn't going down that line at all. That's not to say that I won't change my mind in the future."

Ruth could tell the inspector was intent on playing with her. She inhaled a large breath to calm the anger rising within. "You know as well as I do that it takes a certain type of person to kill someone outright the way Jilly was killed."

"That's as may be. But in my experience, it only takes a person's anger to emerge for a fleeting moment. In that time, the damage has been done, and there is a victim covered in blood. Not only do I have that in this case, but I also discovered your friend standing outside the room where the crime took place, covered in the victim's blood. Can you see where I'm going with this?"

"To be brutally honest with you, no! I can't, because *in my experience,* the perpetrator of a crime rarely hangs around the crime scene, waiting for the police to show up." *Touché. Stick that where the sun don't shine, Inspector.*

Littlejohn glared at her. "All right, if we go along with your line of thinking, why don't you share with me what's running through your mind at present?"

Ruth raised her hands. "Seriously, you really should refrain from asking such leading questions."

"Why is that, Miss Morgan?" the inspector challenged through gritted teeth.

Oops, looks like you've prodded the tiger with a stick, girlie! "Because I fear you might not appreciate what the answer will be. Right, here's my take on this. Whether you want to listen to me or not is entirely up to you. While you're wasting your time questioning me, and indeed Steven, the real culprit who committed this atrocious crime is getting away."

"Is that right? You seem adamant that your friend isn't involved, in spite of the evidence so far proving otherwise. Here's *my* take on it. Steven Swanson was mightily ticked off with the way Ms. Bramley treated him. During the course of the evening, he put on a show for his friends, letting them know that everything was okay with him. Then, once the awards were handed out, Ms. Bramley asked to see Steven in one of the hotel rooms. His mind must have been whirring, going over what the dreadful woman had put him through this week, probably despising the condescending way she'd spoken to him, and saw it as an opportune moment to exact his revenge."

All the way through the inspector's ludicrous summary of possible events, Ruth sat opposite her, shaking her head. "You're wrong, with a capital W. You don't know Steven like I do. He'd never harm anyone; he has a heart of gold. My take is that someone has set him up."

The inspector roared with laughter. "And why would someone go out of their way to do that, Miss Morgan?"

"You tell me? You're the inspector around here. I'm a mere two-bit PI—your words, if I'm not mistaken, from a previous encounter between us."

"You really can be such a foolish woman at times."

Ruth raised her index finger. "A foolish woman who nine times out of ten manages to solve a crime before you've even had your first meeting with your highly trained team." As soon as the words were aired openly, Ruth wished she could take them back. *So much for trying hard not to rattle her cage, idiot!* Knowing the inspector and her reputation, Ruth realised she'd gone too far and there was only going to be one consequence to her actions. The inspector was sure to come down heavily on Steven unless she apologised and, even then, she feared it might be too late to stop the inspector steamrollering into action.

"I think we're done here. I was hoping we could put our differences aside on this one and possibly put our heads together. Clearly, I was wrong."

Crap! The opportunity had arisen, and I hadn't realised it. Now I've well and truly screwed things up. "Wait, I'm sorry. I'm so used to being defensive around you, I missed the signs that an olive branch was being offered."

The inspector grinned. "I fear your apology has come too late to save your friend." She leaned forward in her chair and uttered quietly, "I hope you'll be able to sleep at night, knowing you'll have Steven's fate on your conscience."

"You really are a piece of work, Inspector. If I didn't know better, I would say you're seeing this as some kind of revenge. A way of getting your own back on me for rubbing your nose in it over the past few years. If that is the case, then shame on you. I'll fight until my very last breath if I have to, if only to prove you wrong."

The inspector rose from her chair. "This interview is now over. If you don't mind leaving the room, I have a prime suspect to interview now."

Her blood boiling, Ruth stood but remained where she was as the pair of them exchanged hateful glances. "You're putting a nail in your coffin if you try and pin this on Steven. I'll do everything in my power to get you kicked off the force. He's an innocent man. I'll prove that in the next few days."

"Making idle threats to the officer in charge of your friend's fate isn't going to help either his or your cause. Leave this room with this warning, Miss Morgan. If I catch you interfering in this case, there will be trouble. Furthermore, if I learn that you've asked your boyfriend to obtain any vital evidence without my authorisation, I'll not only ensure he is thrown off the force, I'll also come after you for your PI licence."

"Whoa! Where the heck has that come from? You can't do that." *So much for offering an olive branch!*

"I think you'll find I'm quite within my rights to do both if you insist on stepping on my toes and interfering with a murder enquiry. You think you're something special—you're not. Now, I'll bid you good evening, Miss Morgan. You have my permission to leave the hotel. In other words, your meddlesome behaviour is no longer required around here. Do you hear me?"

Ruth was eager to shove her middle finger in the woman's face, but she took the moral high ground, nodded and gave the inspector a sickly-sweet smile instead. "Of course. Good evening, Inspector. I hope your case goes well."

The inspector studied her for a moment longer before Ruth flounced out of the room, her heart beating like a runaway express train going down a steep incline.

She wandered back to the group to collect her possessions. "I've been ordered to leave the hotel. James, are you coming with me?"

"Of course. Why? She can't do that."

"Apparently she can. Guys, whatever the inspector says, I will be taking on the case. She cannot prevent me from doing that. Steven is an innocent party in this, and I intend to clear his name. Are you with me?"

The Am-Dram members plus their significant others all cheered.

"We're all with you, Ruth. What about if we meet up at the club tomorrow to formulate a plan?" Hils suggested.

"Good idea. We're due to meet at seven anyway. Shall we stick to that?"

The group members, who all appeared to be dumbstruck by the events, either nodded or raised a thumb.

"Good. Don't lose sleep over this. We'll get Steven's name cleared, I'm sure of that. Goodnight all." She blew them a kiss, tears misting her vision.

James threw an arm around her shoulder and guided her out of the room. "This isn't like you, love. Don't let her get to you."

"I'm not really. I gave as good as I got in there. She threatened to strip you of your job if I asked you to spy for me. She really is a nasty piece of work, isn't she?"

"She is. She gets my back up. I'll just have to try and not get caught." He chuckled and placed a tender kiss on her forehead.

"You're a good man, James." He smiled, and together they walked out of the hotel into the freezing midnight air. "Damn, we should have rung for a taxi."

"I doubt if we'll get one, but I'll try anyway. Oh wait, there's one dropping off down the road. Stay here. I'll see if I can catch him before he takes off."

James ran down the steps of the hotel and skidded a few times on the icy patches on the pavement until he managed to reach the taxi. He jumped in the back, and as the cab turned around, Ruth gingerly made her way down the steps, hanging on tightly to the handrail.

They arrived home and were greeted with a bouncy Ben, desperate to relieve himself after hours of being cooped up. James opened the back door while Ruth filled and boiled the kettle. Once Ben had returned from his excursion and the drinks were made, they all went upstairs to bed, although Ruth stopped off in the living room first to pick up her notebook and pen.

Once they'd got undressed and were sitting up in bed drinking their coffee, James suggested, "Why don't we try and get some sleep now and go through things together in the morning? We've both got the day off."

Ruth smiled at James. "Okay. What's the betting I don't sleep tonight?"

"If you don't sleep, wake me up and we'll go over things together."

She leaned over and kissed him. "You're one in a million."

They finished their drinks and snuggled down for the night, holding each other tightly.

7

----

*A*fter a very restless night, Ruth slipped out of the bed, leaving James gently snoring. She threw on a leisure suit she generally wore around the house and on walks out with Ben and opened the back door to find that the snow had been consistently falling overnight. Ben almost disappeared when he ventured outside.

"Damn, I had every intention of taking you for a walk along the coastal path to try and clear my head. I guess we'll have to rethink that one, matey." She shuddered and pushed the door shut once Ben had rushed back in, only he'd brought a mound of snow in with him. After drying him off and picking up the snow he'd dragged in, Ruth overrode the timer on the boiler, made herself a drink of coffee, and then sat at the kitchen table with Ben close to her feet.

There, on a blank page, she plotted out who she thought had a motive to kill Jilly. She placed Jilly's name prominently in the centre bubble and branched out from there, adding an extra bubble once a name popped into her mind, along with a possible motive. The only problem was that at the moment she only had three names she could insert in the bubbles: Steven, Sian and Megan, all of whom were people she liked. Of course, in the likeable character stakes, Steven would take first place, above the two women she'd only met in the last day or two. She wracked her brain for the next half an hour trying to add further names to the diagram and came up with a big fat blank.

She yelped when James entered the room and placed his arms around her. "Morning, you. Why didn't you wake me? I thought we were going to go over this together?"

"You were having such a lovely sleep, it seemed a shame to wake you. I haven't made much headway anyway, so it's all good. Sit down, I'll fix us some breakfast."

"I'm more than capable of scrambling a few eggs and frying some bacon rashers while you carry on."

She wriggled out of his grasp and stood. "Honestly, I could do with the distraction. I'm at an impasse as it is."

He didn't argue further. Instead, he sat at the table and turned the paper round to have a look. "Are these the people you suspect the most?"

"Yep. There have to be more, I just can't think of any. I really object to putting Steven on that list but I think we have to."

"I agree. Later we can come up with a few ideas as to why we should discount him.

While she cooked the breakfast, James sat at the table jotting down notes. Out of the corner of her eye she saw him pick up his mobile phone, read the screen and shake his head slowly. "Anything of interest?"

James sighed and swivelled in his chair to face her. "It's the BBC news alert, the local one. You're not going to like this, love."

Frowning, she lowered the gas and joined him. He held the phone up so she could read the message for herself.

Local man arrested for the murder of celebrity author Jilly Bramley.

*S*tunned to the core, Ruth sank into her chair and reread the words on the screen. She glanced up at James and shrugged. "This has floored me. I just don't know how to react, not without using expletives anyway. That inspector is a ...well, I'll leave you to fill in the blanks.

James reached across the table and wrapped both hands around hers. "We'll get to the bottom of this, Ruth. I'll help you all I can."

"How? She specifically pointed out that if you interfered you'd be sacked. We can't risk that. We need your income to keep us afloat when my business is slow."

"I know. But I can't sit back and watch them arrest an innocent man."

"What can we do about it?" Ruth asked, surprising even herself when she uttered the words. Usually, there was no stopping her when she felt an injustice had been served.

James smiled. "You can finish cooking the breakfast, and then we'll continue to do what we planned on doing: writing a list of possible suspects and their likely motives. And then I think we should take a trip to the hotel and start asking some questions of our own."

"But it's a crime scene. It'll probably be shut off to the public, won't it? At least for the next day or two."

A twinkle developed in his eye. "You're grief-stricken and desperate to share your condolences with Jilly's family and friends, aren't you?"

She left her seat and ruffled his hair on the way back to the stove. "You're not just a pretty face after all."

"Gee, thanks. Do you want me to take Ben out after breakfast while you get ready? The sooner we get down to the hotel the better."

"That would be smashing. Okay, all the doom and gloom has dissipated now. Our main aim is to question everyone at the hotel who was either at that party or serving the guests last night."

A low whistle left James' lips. "That could take us weeks. We need to narrow that list down to friends and family for now."

"Okay, maybe I'm guilty of letting my enthusiasm get the better of me there. Perhaps you should rephrase that to friends, family *and foes* in that case."

"Ah, I get where you're going. It would appear she'd made a number of enemies over the last few days at the hotel. We just need to put a name to those people and ask the right questions."

Ruth withdrew two plates from the cupboard and dished up the breakfast as the toast popped up. "That's going to be really tough, unless people are willing to add names to our suspect list. Every time I entered the hallway last night, I heard her shouting at someone. I haven't got a clue who the recipients of her anger were, though. Do you really think people are going to admit they were at the wrong end of a tongue-lashing, aware that the police could bring them in for questioning?"

"I understand what you're saying, but you're a pro. You have a knack of getting people to confide in you. If we go down that route rather than go in there all guns blazing, demanding answers, I'm sure we'll come up with something significant that could lead to Steven's release."

She placed the two plates on the table and sat there staring at the contents for a short while before she finally picked up her cutlery and got stuck in. She was eating out of necessity, to keep her strength up for what lay ahead of her, not because she was particularly hungry.

They ate their breakfast in silence, the only sound coming from under the table where Ben was. He always moaned while they ate, as if to say, 'Hey, don't forget about me. Ever the hungry hound down here'.

Ruth smirked and pushed aside some bacon to give him after they'd finished. She had a rule that denied either of them feeding Ben off their plates during a meal. To do that would have meant he'd stare at them and beg, drooling in anticipation. She loved her beloved dog dearly; however, she couldn't abide him keeping his beady eye on them, waiting for scraps. Other people might think it cute, but she didn't. There were boundaries that needed clearly defining. Admittedly, there weren't many because she treated Ben as if he was a four-legged human most of the time.

With their breakfast completed and the dishes washed and dried,

James stuck to his word and took Ben out for a walk in the snow, giving Ruth the opportunity to grab a quick shower and get dressed. She was ready to roll when she heard the pair enter the back door.

"I'll be down in a second, just adding a touch of makeup."

"You don't need that muck sitting on your face, you're beautiful enough as it is," James shouted up from the bottom of the stairs.

She descended the stairs with a smile. He sure knew how and when to make her feel good about herself. She found herself getting excited at the prospect of parading around with the engagement ring he had mentioned he would be purchasing soon. *Would it really be that bad to take the plunge and marry him? We live together as it is. He's cleaner than most men around the house. Does his share with the chores and brings a pretty decent wage in to boot.* Maybe she should take a few days out to write down the pros and cons of being married to him. *Would it be fair to do that? To treat my future as if it were some kind of business decision?*

She was busy thinking over the questions and almost lost her footing near the bottom step.

James reached out his arms to save her. "Hey, steady. Are you still suffering from the effects of supping all that prosecco last night?"

"Hardly. Miles away. I'll be more careful next time. Are you ready to head over to the hotel?"

"As I'll ever be. Let's hope the dreaded she-devil isn't around to prevent us from carrying out our plan."

"I was hoping the same. There's only one way to find out." She patted Ben on the head and instructed, "Go and lie in your bed, boy. We'll be back soon."

"I'll ring Mrs Sanders later to ask her to let him out if we get held up."

With his head bowed low, Ben wandered through the hallway and into the kitchen. Ruth's heart developed a slight twinge; he usually went everywhere with her. Aware that they would need to walk to the hotel in the snow and that they wouldn't allow him in once they arrived, there was no alternative but to leave him here. At least he'd be warm now the boiler was up and running once more. She was thankful for small mercies on that front.

When they arrived at the hotel, they tapped the snow off their boots and entered the foyer to find David Strong, the hotel manager, speaking to the young girl on reception. Ruth and James approached the desk.

"Hello, David. Have things calmed down yet?"

He shrugged, the dark half-circles under his eyes telling Ruth the poor man hadn't managed to sleep well. "Not sure what you mean by *calmed down*, Ruth."

"Sorry, have the police gone now, or is it too soon to think that?"

"There's still crime scene tape draped across the hallway. It's caused no end of trouble with the guests. We had to use one of the small conference rooms as a dining hall this morning. Many of them were unimpressed, I can tell you."

"Oh heck, poor you. You'd think the guests would understand your dilemma in the circumstances, wouldn't you?"

"People paying good money expect the best, I suppose. We normally go the extra mile to tend to their every need. Anyway, enough about my problems. What can I do for you?"

"Well, as you know, I run the local detective agency and I'm a qualified PI. We were wondering if you wouldn't mind letting us question the staff and possibly a few of the guests."

He tilted his head to the right. "I knew you were a PI, but as to you questioning people, wouldn't the inspector in charge of the case raise an objection to you doing that?"

"She could do, but I still have a right to search for the truth. You know how much Steven means to the community. I've been instructed by the Am-Dram club members to try to solve the case."

"Whoa! So they have a fund for this type of thing? How cool is that?"

Ruth fixed a grin in place, hoping he wouldn't be able to pick up the fact that she was telling a white lie. It was in a good cause after all. "I know! Isn't it wonderful when a community rallies around and comes together in the face of adversity?"

"Definitely. All right, in that case it would be foolish of me to deny you access to all areas, except the cordoned-off part, of course."

"If the inspector shows up, can we come to some agreement about what we should say if she asks why I'm, sorry, why we're on-site?"

"Do you think that'll be necessary?" he asked, suddenly appearing to be a little worried about stepping on the inspector's toes.

"Possibly. I'd like to go down the route that we're here to pay our respects to the family, if that's all right. We'll conduct our investigation discreetly, I promise you. You know James is in the force, yes?"

"I thought he was. Well, then, I can't see any harm in letting you in to conduct your interviews. I was puzzled to see the inspector hadn't shown up this morning to resume her interviews. When she left in the small hours of this morning, around two, I believe it was, she didn't mention she'd be back today. Maybe now that she's arrested Steven, she thinks she can take her foot off the gas."

"You know he didn't do it?" Ruth replied without hesitation.

"I don't know anything of the sort. If he didn't do it, how do you explain him being covered in the woman's blood?"

"He stumbled across her after the murder had been committed. I was there when Jilly summoned him. He innocently left the banqueting room to join her. Perhaps someone knew that and pounced on the opportunity to do away with her and point the finger at an innocent bystander." *Whoa! Is that what truly happened? Someone set Steven up?*

James tugged her arm and widened his eyes as if inferring she'd said too much already.

She nodded and added, "Of course, that's pure speculation on my part at this very early stage in the enquiry. Tell me, is Jilly's entourage still here?"

"Yes. None of them showed up for breakfast this morning."

The receptionist coughed. "Sorry to dispute that, sir, but Mr Baker had breakfast at his usual time, just after nine."

"Ah, I wasn't aware of that. I stand corrected, Maria, thank you."

"No sign of the daughter, Fiona?"

"No sign of any of the others this morning. I've been on duty since seven," the receptionist told them.

"Interesting. I wonder if it would be possible to question the staff who were on duty during the evening."

"There's a few around, and others will be in for their shift later. I have to tell you that we also took on a few agency staff for the event."

"I didn't realise that. I don't suppose you have a list that we can go from? It would definitely help to make things run smoother."

"I can sort that out for you. It might take me half an hour or so."

"That's fine. Would it be possible to start interviewing the staff you have on duty in the meantime?"

"Of course. The temporary dining room should have been cleared by now. Why don't I send them in to you one by one? How's that?"

"Excellent. I really do appreciate your cooperation. It should make things go swimmingly."

"Always happy to lend a hand where I think someone's life is in jeopardy. From what I could tell, having observed the two of you at work together this week, Steven seems a nice man. He went above and beyond to get this foyer set up, as did you. My question would be, why on earth would he do that and then kill the person he busted a gut to please?"

Ruth winked at him and pointed a finger. "That's what I'm thinking. It just doesn't make sense. Which is why I'm going to dig deep to uncover the truth."

"You have my full backing. Although that will have to be done discreetly if the inspector shows up. I've heard she has a mean streak and I'd be reluctant to get on the wrong side of her, if you get my drift."

Ruth and James both chuckled, then Ruth said, "We hear you, David. Shall we make our way into the conference room then?"

David pointed out the room, which was just off the hallway, as a grey-haired man with a snowy-white beard entered the lobby.

Ruth didn't recognise the man from the event the previous evening. She pretended to speak to James about something, intent on eavesdropping on the conversation.

"Ah, that's right. I'm delighted to meet you, Mr Bramley. Please accept my condolences on the loss of your wife," David stated with genuine feeling in his voice.

Ruth's interest piqued, and she raised an eyebrow at James. He tugged on her arm, urging her to go with him. But Ruth refused to move until she'd heard more.

"That's *ex*-wife," Mr Bramley stiffly corrected David.

"Oh my! Of course, I'm so sorry. Can I get someone to collect your bags from your car?"

"No. I won't be staying. I'm on a flying visit to support my daughter. I have no intention of hanging around in this dive longer than necessary. I'm sorry, that was rude of me. I'm upset and angry, as you can imagine."

"Of course. I'll ring your daughter's room immediately. If you'd care to take a seat."

"We should go, Ruth," James whispered in her ear.

"No, I want to hang around, see what happens when they meet up. He seems very standoffish to me."

"What are you like? He's probably grieving. Even if she was his ex-wife, he must have loved her at one time. They begat a daughter."

Ruth tried hard to suppress a giggle at his choice of words. "Begat? Where the hell did that come from? Let's wait over here."

She clawed his arm, and they moved to the far side of the lobby, where they pretended to study the tourist information on offer, and awaited Fiona's arrival.

Within five minutes the lift *pinged,* and Fiona and her boyfriend emerged. Fiona ran at full speed into her father's outstretched arms. He soothed a hand over her head and down her back and extended a hand to shake Jake's.

Ruth lifted a brochure to chest level and observed the three of them. She was close enough to hear what was being said, which was an added bonus.

"Dad, it was dreadful. Who would do such a thing? I'm so pleased you're here. Jake's done his best to help me to try and make sense of what happened, but neither of us know much. The policewoman in charge of the case arrested the set designer." She extracted herself from her father's arms and motioned at the display surrounding them. "He did all this, for her, then killed her."

"Hey, let's be fair about this, Fi," Jake interjected. "He was pretty upset about having to strip it all down and start all over again. He had the motive. That's all the inspector would've needed to have made the arrest." As if sensing Ruth was in the same room, Jake turned to face her and smiled awkwardly.

Ruth took that as an opportunity to introduce herself. After placing the brochure back in the rack, she crossed the room, James close beside her. She extended her hand to Mr Bramley. "Hello, sir. I'm Ruth Morgan. I actually helped Steven Swanson create the set."

Mr Bramley refused to shake her hand; instead, he pulled his daughter protectively towards him. "Why are you here?"

Ruth smiled, trying to cut through the icy atmosphere that had developed. "Steven is a dear friend of mine. I assure you he's innocent."

Mr Bramley frowned. "Wait, how do you know that? Were you here last night?"

"Yes. Let me say further that I'm also the local private investigator." She paused to let the information sink in.

Both Fiona and Jake seemed shocked by the revelation.

"Anyway, the townsfolk have contributed to fund my investigation. I have every intention of clearing Steven's name. Furthermore, I have a decent track record for uncovering the truth where the local police fail."

"I don't believe in private investigators, Ms. Morgan. I don't see the point in them, not when we have a perfectly adequate police force on hand. If you'll excuse me, I've come here specifically to see my daughter, not to stand around idly chatting with all and sundry."

He turned his back, shielding Fiona in the process. Jake shrugged when Ruth pleaded with him.

Determined not to give up that easily, Ruth smiled. "I understand. Fiona, would it be possible to have a quick word with you in a little while? I'll probably be here most of the day, questioning the staff and the other guests who stayed at the hotel last night."

"That's utterly absurd. I won't allow it. I've already told you that your type isn't wanted around here. Can't you see how upset she is? Have some compassion, woman, for Pete's sake."

Ruth inhaled a large breath and took a step back. "I'm sorry. All I'm trying to do is ensure that justice is served correctly. Right now, an innocent man is being blamed for your ex-wife's murder."

Jake snorted. "He's hardly innocent. His motive must be the most prominent. We could all see how angry he was when Jilly ripped his efforts to bits."

"I agree he was angry earlier, but during the evening he'd accepted that Jilly wasn't a great admirer of his work and moved on. I can assure you, he's as innocent as a newborn kitten," Ruth countered, her heart racing.

James stepped forward and tugged on Ruth's arm. "Come on, Ruth, leave them to grieve in peace."

He was right. She was pushing too hard and too soon. They needed time to get used to the idea that Jilly was dead. "Perhaps you'll reconsider in a few days. I'll leave you my card."

Ruth slipped one of her business cards into Fiona's jacket pocket, much to her father's disgust. He grunted and led his sobbing daughter, accompanied by Jake, back to the lift. Ruth stood there and watched as the doors slid shut behind them.

"Right, well, that's the end of that. I doubt if the father is going to allow Fiona to speak to us anytime soon. Without that conversation taking place, I think our job just got that little bit harder, not that it was going to be that easy in the first place."

They walked into the conference room, which had been cleared, and arranged for their use by the two members of staff on duty, a blonde woman and a man in his early twenties.

"Thanks so much for doing this." Ruth smiled.

"Our pleasure. Would you like a drink? I can bring you a tea or coffee," the young woman asked.

"A coffee would be wonderful, for both of us. You're very kind. A quick question if I may? Were either of you on duty last night?"

They both nodded, then the young woman replied, "It was a shocking thing to happen. We've never had anything as bad as that go on here. The most we've ever seen is someone arguing over their bill. But to have a death, sorry, a murder at the hotel, well…" She shuddered, unable to say more when tears formed in her eyes.

"I know, it is tough. Would you both be willing to have a brief chat with me? Obviously, you'll need to check with your manager first, but if he gives you the all clear, would you?"

The couple looked at each other and nodded.

"Sure," the woman said. "Let me get the drinks sorted and ask the boss. Chris, do you want to finish clearing the cutlery tray et cetera from the end table for me? Then that'll be us finished."

"Wonderful. We'll see you soon." Ruth pulled out a chair at the nearby table and sat. She withdrew her notebook and pen and started jotting down some notes.

James joined her and leaned over to have a peep. "What did you make of the father?"

"In what way?" she asked, puzzled.

"I felt he was being a tad overprotective perhaps," James replied, lowering his voice.

"Seriously? The thought never occurred to me. If a member of your family had been through a similar ordeal, wouldn't you react the same way?"

"Maybe. Oh, I don't know. Let's just say that something didn't sit well with me out there."

Ruth mulled his statement over for a few seconds and dismissed it with a shake of her head. "Okay, I think you're wrong but I'm going to go along with your notion and delve into his past a bit. Did you hear him say that he had no intention of staying overnight? He must live locally then, right?"

"Yep, I caught that."

"Judging by your tone, you're suspicious of him."

James shrugged. "Aren't you? There's something not quite adding up, and I can't put my finger on what that is yet. All I'm saying is, you shouldn't discount him in your investigation."

"Oh, I won't, don't worry. Everyone in this hotel is a suspect in my book until I've spoken to them. I get the impression this is going to be one of my toughest cases to date."

James chuckled. "You always say that on the first day of the investigation until things slot into place."

"I know, but I mean it this time. Ah, here's our coffee now."

The young woman placed a tray with a pot of coffee and two cups and saucers on the table beside Ruth. "Here you go. The boss has given us permission to speak to you before we continue with our duties, or do you want to have your coffee first?"

"Brilliant news. James, will you pour the drinks while I start?"

James did as requested.

"Sorry," Ruth said. "I didn't catch your name."

The young woman sat opposite Ruth, while Chris held back and stood by the doorway. Ruth gestured for him to join them.

"It's Sharon Hardcastle."

Chris sat next to Sharon.

"Can I have your full name, Chris?"

"Chris O'Brien."

Ruth smiled, trying to put the anxious couple at ease. "Are you Irish?"

"That's right, although my parents moved to England back in the sixties. I've only stepped foot in Ireland once over the years. I keep meaning to go back for a visit but never seem to manage to squeeze it in what with working full time. Our shifts can be erratic in the hotel business."

"I can imagine. Although working here should keep you on an even keel, shouldn't it? I mean, this place always seems exceptionally busy to me."

He shrugged. "Depends what events are on and if there are any murders taking place." He grinned when Sharon slapped his thigh.

Ruth sensed the couple were much more than just work associates. "Have you been dating long?"

Sharon's cheeks flared up. "A few weeks. I was fed up with his constant badgering me for a date and eventually gave in. The boss has no idea, though. If you could keep it a secret, we'd appreciate it."

Ruth pulled an imaginary zip across her lips. "I won't utter a word. Do your shifts always coincide?"

"Mostly, that's how we got together," Sharon replied, shyly turning to face Chris.

"Okay, so you were both on duty last night. Can I ask where you were? I don't recall seeing either of you working in the banqueting suite."

"I was flitting in and out. I helped to set up for the function and then offered to help out in the kitchen as a few members of staff had called in sick—well, not really sick, they live out in the sticks and were afraid of getting cut off by the snow," Sharon informed her.

"It was ghastly weather last night, even worse today. Do you both live locally?"

"In the next village. Lunder. Chris's dad has a four-by-four. If it wasn't for him suggesting we use it, we couldn't have got in. Staffing levels are worse today. I think at the last count we're at least ten staff members down, which is sending the manager into a spin."

"Understandable. We'll try not to keep you from your duties too long. I'll get to the point. Did you happen to either see or overhear anything last night?"

"To do with the crime?" Sharon asked, her brow forming a frown.

"Yes."

"Not really. Like I said, at the suspected time it happened, I was knee-deep in washing dishes in the kitchen."

Ruth turned to Chris. "What about you, Chris?"

"Nothing. I was going hell for leather last night. The boss had me stocking up the bar, running errands for him, liaising with the other staff members, not only in the banqueting hall but also in the kitchen, ensuring the food and drink flowed freely during the event. It was full-on, I can tell you."

Ruth nodded. "So I saw. James had to stand in and help last night, too. He volunteered to play with the band when the drummer fell ill."

Chris clicked his fingers. "I knew I recognised you. You did an outstanding job. I had a drum kit when I was a teenager. My mum gave it away, said she couldn't stand the noise and that it was the worst Christmas present she'd ever bought me. I didn't have a lot of say in the matter. I miss pounding out a beat, though. Might invest in another kit in the future."

"You should. I hear it's a good way to make a living," James replied.

Ruth cleared her throat, hating to interrupt their conversation; however, she was desperate to hear what the couple knew, if anything. "Perhaps you overheard something in the hallway when you were rushing between the different areas?"

Chris's gaze drifted for a moment or two then returned to Ruth. "I do recall a lot of shouting going on. If I remember rightly, it was all kicking off at the most hectic time of the evening, when we were setting up."

"Before the awards took place and the murder was committed?" Ruth asked.

"Yes. I don't think I heard anything else later on in the evening. Would any of us? Wasn't she stabbed?"

"It's the argument side of things I'm more interested in. Someone was angry enough to kill her. My job is to figure out who that person is."

"Sorry, I can't help you further. All the arguments I heard were earlier, before eight."

"Not to worry. Can you remember how you learned about the death?"

Chris shrugged. "One of the waitresses came running into the kitchen to say she'd seen a man leaning against the wall, covered in blood. My supervisor ran into the reception area to track down the manager. He called the police right away. Everyone was in a flap then. We didn't know what to do for the best. The chef warned us to keep out of the way until the police showed up."

"That was a wise move. The person you saw covered in blood is my friend. I saw him in the hallway and stayed with him until the police arrived. I know deep down that my friend is innocent. Jilly Bramley requested his company, that's when he discovered she was dead. The reason he was covered in blood was because he did what any one of us would do if we found ourselves in the same situation—he tried to help in some small way. It backfired on him, and now he's been arrested for Jilly's murder." Ruth realised she had tears running down her cheeks.

James placed a hand over hers. "It's all right, love. We'll find the culprit."

She swiped away the tears with the cuff of her jacket. "I'm so sorry. You can see how emotional I am about this. My friend could be put away for life if he's found guilty. I have to help him. He's an innocent party in all this, and I'm determined to get to the truth."

Sharon bowed her head and mumbled, "That's awful. Surely, isn't it up to the police to question people who were on duty last night?"

"It should be, yes. However, over the years, the inspector in charge of the case and I haven't exactly seen eye to eye. I want to do all I can to ensure every angle is covered, without stepping on the inspector's toes, of course."

"I think I would try and do the same if any of my friends were caught up in such a dreadful situation," Sharon said, raising her head to look at Ruth. She, too, had tears welling up.

"If neither of you heard or saw anything untoward, perhaps you know of someone who did? Maybe another of your colleagues mentioned something in passing?"

Chris and Sharon glanced at each other and shook their heads.

Chris answered the question. "No, sorry. We'd tell you if we knew anything."

Sensing she was wasting time now, Ruth decided it would be best if she dismissed the couple and moved on to someone else. "One last question before I let you go. Have either of you seen the rest of Ms. Bramley's entourage this morning? Her publicist or agent?"

Sharon nodded. "Yes, they both came down to the lobby around eight. I thought they were going to have breakfast but when I offered to get them something to eat, they both said they couldn't face it and returned to their rooms. They appeared distraught to me."

"Understandable in the circumstances. At least they're still around. Okay, thank you, Chris and Sharon, you're free to get on with your duties now."

The young couple smiled and left their seats.

"I sense this is all going to be a waste of time," James admitted, watching Sharon and Chris leave.

Ruth sighed. "Me, too. Where should we turn to help Steven then? I'm up to suggestions."

"Haven't got a Scooby Doo."

The rest of the staff filed in for questioning, and after a couple of hours of mind-numbingly repeating the same questions over and over again, Ruth was on the verge of giving up when one of the waitresses hinted at something of interest.

Rachel Kennett, a waitress in her early thirties, seemed to hesitate when she sat at the table.

"Hello, Rachel, there's really no need for you to be nervous. A little background knowledge for you before we begin. I'm the local private investigator based in the town. This is my partner, James. We're questioning the staff about the shocking incident that happened last night. You're aware of that, right?"

"Yes, everyone knows there was a murder here last night. Not sure why you want to question me, though." She shifted in her seat.

Interest radar on full alert, Ruth issued the woman her best smile, trying to place her at ease. "We're asking every member of staff if they either saw or heard anything while they were on duty. Did you?"

"Not really, no."

"Not really? Are you saying you did?"

The woman's hands clenched and unclenched on the table in front of her. "Well, I might have overheard something."

"Which was? You won't get into trouble if you tell us, I assure you."

"Won't I? I'm not keen on snitching on my fellow workers."

"Let us be the judge of that. Anything you say to us now will be classed as confidential. Please tell us?"

"All right. Look, I don't know if it's going to be of use or not, but here goes. One of the waiters, Darren Broadstairs, had a crush on Jilly Bramley."

Ruth let out the large breath she was holding on to. "I think a few people had a crush on her. I know my friend's boss attended the event last night only because he'd been an admirer of Jilly's for years."

"Okay, there's being an admirer, but is that the same as someone who you think is obsessed?"

Intrigued, Ruth tilted her head. "Can you tell us what you mean by obsessed?"

"As soon as Darren heard that Jilly had booked the hotel, he went into excited mode. He had a word with the manager, insisted he was on every shift during her stay. That type of thing."

"Did he meet her? As in, talk to her?"

"I think he tried. Told me that when he was helping to set up the banqueting room for the award event, she looked right past him as though he didn't exist. He spoke to her, and she didn't even have the decency to respond."

"I see. That must have ticked him off."

Rachel shrugged, her mouth turned down at the sides. "Me, I'd be pretty angry, but Darren seemed to accept it because she was a celebrity."

"Is Darren on duty today?"

"No, he rang in sick this morning."

"Did he now? What about last night? Was he on duty when the murder occurred?"

"Yes. I had to console him. He was going out of his mind, acting like a crazy man. I felt so sorry for him. I wasn't surprised when he didn't show up for work this morning."

"What a shame. We'll make a note to call round and see him, make sure he's coping all right after the shock he's received. Is there anything else you can tell us, Rachel?"

She pondered the question for a second then shook her head. "No, I don't think so." She glanced over her shoulder at the door and then back at Ruth and James. Leaning forward, she whispered, "I could keep my ear to the ground for you, for a cost."

"Cost? You want us to pay you for information?" James screeched.

Ruth tapped his leg under the table with her own. "I'm afraid my business isn't doing well enough to pay for information, Rachel. I'll give you my card. If you hear anything you think might benefit the investigation, would you contact me?"

Rachel picked up the card and thrust it down her bra. "I might do. Is that it? Can I go now?"

Feeling deflated, Ruth nodded. "Yes, you may go."

Rachel left the room.

"What a cheeky mare!" James hissed.

Ruth sniggered. "I suppose there was bound to be one. Some people see divulging information as topping up their insignificant wages. I tend to pity folks like that."

"Are you telling me this type of thing goes on all the time?"

"Not all the time. But yes, I have been asked to line a person's palm with silver, or a twenty, on more than one occasion."

"Wow, the nerve of folks really is beyond me at times. No wonder some people refuse to speak to the police if that's their intention. Gone are the days when we used informers and paid for the information they had to offer."

"Rightly so. People have no morals these days. If I had valuable news about a murder, I'd be on the phone immediately."

"It's shameful. Anyway, do you think it'll be worth chasing this Darren up?"

"Definitely, don't you? From what Rachel told us, I'm willing to put his name on the suspect list. Strange that he hasn't turned in for work today. Would that be because of guilt?"

"Flipping that on its head, it might be because he was devastated to hear of Jilly's death. We could be condemning an innocent man for the way he reacted to her death."

Ruth raised an eyebrow and looked James in the eye. "Isn't that what Littlejohn has done to Steven?"

"I suppose so. We've been at it for hours, why don't we take a break? Have a bite to eat?"

"I agree. I'll see if the manager will lay on some sandwiches for us. Be right back." Ruth walked into the lobby and headed for the reception desk.

Maria was in the process of checking out one of the guests. The customer handed over his credit card to complete the transaction then left the hotel.

"Hi, is there any chance we could get a couple of sandwiches? Or is that imposing too much?"

Maria smiled. "No, that's fine. We usually have a bar menu on the go. Any idea what you fancy?"

"A couple of cheese and ham sandwiches would be lovely, thank you."

"Would you like another pot of coffee to go with them?"

"If you wouldn't mind?"

"Not at all. I'll place the order and be back in a jiffy."

True to her word, the receptionist was only gone a few moments before she returned. "I've placed the order. I'll get a member of staff to bring it in to you."

"I was wondering if it would be okay if we ate out here, you know, for a change of scenery."

"I don't see why not. How's it all going in there?"

Ruth held her hand up and waved it from side to side. "Hit and miss, if you must know. I'm not sure how many other people there are to see this afternoon, but we've got a few leads to follow up on, so it's not all been a waste of time."

"Excellent news. I know the man they arrested, your friend, had a tough time with Ms. Bramley, but surely that wouldn't have resulted in him killing her, would it? Even if he was tempted, he'd hardly hang around at the scene, waiting for someone to find him. That's my take on it, for what it's worth."

"You're right. That's the logic I'm trying to adapt to the case. Not only that, I know Steven of old, and he just doesn't have it in him to kill someone, no matter how badly they treated him. It takes a certain kind of person to take someone's life."

"I think you're right. Why do you think the police are digging their heels in?"

"That's what this particular inspector is good at. Did you have much to do with Jilly?"

"Not really. I generally deal with either her publicist or her agent."

"Any idea when they'll be leaving? I'd like a word with them before they go and would hate to miss the opportunity."

"They haven't told us openly yet; however, they have hinted that it'll be in the next few days. It probably depends on the police investigation. What I find strange is that you're here questioning the staff and yet the police aren't. Does that type of thing happen a lot?"

"Only with specific cases. Mainly the ones Inspector Littlejohn deals with."

"That's appalling. How does she get away with that?"

"I think because in the past, I have solved a few of the crimes and she's taken the credit for the arrests."

The receptionist's jaw hung open for a moment or two. "What? Can she do that?"

"I got used to it. At the end of the day, my conscience is clear, and I don't have trouble sleeping. I'm wondering if she can say the same."

"I know if I stabbed someone in the back like that, it would play on my mind. May I ask what made you become a PI?"

Ruth smiled and scratched the side of her head. "I wanted to do the right thing. Be there for people who need help solving things that are bugging them. It's not as glamorous as you think it is. Sometimes I have to climb trees or hide down dark alleys in the pouring rain if I'm following someone."

"What would you say your main cases are?"

"I suppose the usual suspects, cheating spouses, male and female nowadays. The odd murder thrown in. You heard about the murder up at Carmel Cove Hall, I take it?"

Maria nodded.

"The victim was my best friend's new husband. I solved the crime before the police investigation really got underway."

"How?"

"Tenacity. At the end of the day, I only ask the obvious questions. Questions that the police should be asking but omit to. Shh…I should have said that quietly—my fiancé is a copper."

"Ouch! That must have benefits, though."

"Sometimes it does. He's one of the good ones. I'd love him to work with me one day. I think we'd make an excellent team. Don't tell him I said that. At the moment, the business is just starting out and wouldn't be able to sustain two people's wages."

"That's a shame. Maybe that'll change soon. Hey, why don't you leave some cards with me? You never know when a guest might need a super sleuth to solve a mystery."

Ruth sniggered and handed over a wad of cards. "That's very kind of you."

One of the waiters Ruth had already spoken to appeared and stopped at the reception desk.

"Looks like your lunch has arrived. Why don't you put it on the table over there for Miss Morgan, Chris?"

"Thanks. We'll eat this and get back to it. How much do I owe?"

The kind receptionist winked. "I'll sort this for you, don't worry."

Ruth was floored by her generosity. "You don't have to do that."

"I know I don't. Eat, it'll be fine. Give me a shout if you need anything else."

"Gosh, I'd be too embarrassed to ask for anything further. Thank you."

Ruth dipped into the conference room to fetch James. He was busy making notes but rushed to join her as soon as she mentioned that the food had arrived.

8

They ate their meal and summarised the sparse information they had gathered that morning. Ruth was just about to place the final piece of her sandwich in her mouth when the lift doors opened. Out stepped Fiona and her father. Neither of them glanced their way. Fiona hugged her father tightly at the door and watched him walk down the steps to his car. She turned, her head bowed, and made her way back to the lift.

Ruth seized the opportunity to have a word. "Hello, Fiona. How are you?"

She sighed. "How do you think I am? I'm sorry, that was rude of me. What do you want?"

"A brief chat, if you wouldn't mind?"

"About what? My mother's murder?"

Ruth winced at the ferociousness behind her reply. "Yes," she said bluntly. "As you know, I'm investigating the case and wondered if you had any thoughts on who you think might have done it."

"Let me mull that over for a second. Done. The man the police have in custody. I really don't understand why you're interfering in the case when the riddle has already been solved. Oh wait, of course, the man is a friend of yours and you believe him to be innocent, am I correct?"

"Well, yes. I have my reasons for believing in Steven. I know the evidence points at him killing your mother, but seriously, do you really believe that? If he'd committed the crime, wouldn't he have legged it? Left the scene before anyone else came along? He didn't. Instead, when I found him, he was in shock and unable to move."

"Maybe the shock of committing the crime lay heavy on him and he froze once he'd done the deed."

"I doubt that was the case, otherwise he would have still been inside the room."

"Whatever. All I know is someone has been arrested for killing my beautiful mother. Yes, she had her faults over the years, but doesn't everyone? I will miss her dearly."

"I'm sure you will. Please, if you can spare me a few minutes, I'd like to ask you if you know of anyone who might have had a grudge against your mother and who you'd put in the frame for killing her."

She laughed hard. "Doh! That points to your friend again. He was angry when she told him to redesign this place, even you have to admit that much."

"I do admit it. However, I know in my heart that Steven isn't capable of ending someone's life, accidentally or otherwise."

"Some might say you're guilty of being biased."

"Maybe. But I'm willing to put my business on the line to prove he's innocent. He has no reason to lie to me, Miss Bramley, I can assure you. Also, if I had one teeny doubt about his innocence, I wouldn't have taken on the investigation in the first place."

"Is that right?" Fiona said, her reply dripping in sarcasm.

"Yes. You'll have to take my word on that. Please, just sit down with me for five minutes to go over a few possibilities."

She paced the area and then finally gave a defeated shrug. "Five minutes. Jake is waiting for me. We're going to leave later today."

"So soon? Why is that?"

"Jake has to get back to work. I've said I'll go with him. There's very little I can do around here anyway."

Ruth pointed to the seating area where she'd eaten lunch. "I understand. Would you like to speak here or in private in the conference room?"

"Let's go in there."

James followed Ruth and Fiona into the conference room. They each took a seat at the table. Ruth opened her notebook to a clean page.

"You seem to have been busy." Fiona motioned at the notes sitting beside James.

"Yes and no. A lot of it is repeated. I think we've questioned every member of staff now."

"Who's next, apart from me?"

"A few of the guests who attended the event last night, your boyfriend, Sian and Megan."

"I don't think Sian, Megan or Jake will be able to help you at all."

"Maybe you can tell us what your relationship is like with Sian and Megan?"

"Fine. I don't really have that much to do with them."

"And they got on well with your mother?"

She laughed. "Not really, but that's the world we live in, isn't it? They both tolerated Mum."

"So are you telling me things have been bad between them for a while?"

"Years would be the answer to that one. I think both women were on the verge of jacking in their jobs. Mum was always sacking them. Let me rephrase that, she threatened one minute to sack them and rescinded it the next."

"How did Sian and Megan react to that?"

"I doubt they were very happy, but they accepted Mum for who she was. Her celebrity status turned her into a diva most of the time. You were on the end of her sharp tongue, I believe?"

"I was. I gave as good as I got. Your mother didn't frighten me."

Fiona chortled. "She must have lost her touch then, because usually anyone who spoke back to her ended up a quivering wreck."

"Like Steven?" Ruth suggested, reading Fiona's mind.

She grinned as if she'd made her point already and there was no need to mention his name further. "I truly don't see why you're wasting your time questioning other people when there is already someone in custody."

"As I've already stated, I believe the police have arrested the wrong man. My aim is to right that wrong."

"Good luck. To me, the writing, or blood as it was, is on the wall for your friend. If you're looking for motives, then he was a prime candidate, or are you denying that?"

"Perhaps I'd be inclined to agree with you if I didn't know Steven well. As things stand, he's a man of integrity who goes above and beyond for this community."

"He also has a vile temper, according to my mother."

"Is that so? Well, I was here working with him the forty-eight hours before your mother's death and saw no sign of that. He worked tirelessly to get this place looking stunning. Even when your mother distastefully rejected his attempt to make amends, I wouldn't say his anger boiled over."

"Miss Morgan, the only thing distasteful about what's happened in the past twenty-four hours, apart from that godawful set design, is that my mother's life has ended. Now, if you'll excuse me, I have a suitcase to pack. I don't see the sense in us going round and round in circles." Fiona stood and stared down at Ruth, her eyes challenging her to say something else.

"Okay, all that's left for me to say is thank you for your time and to wish you a safe trip."

"Thank you. My advice would be to take the rest of the day off, it is Sunday after all, and leave the investigation to the police. They seem to have their finger on the pulse so far, as they've arrested your friend. Goodbye." Fiona flounced out of the room, giving the impression that she'd inherited some of her mother's diva genes.

Ruth sat back in her chair, shaking her head.

"What's wrong?" James asked.

"My gut is telling me something doesn't sit right with that one."

"I think your gut is wrong. Leave the poor girl alone, she's grieving the death of her mother."

"Maybe or maybe not." She waved her hand in front of her and sat forward again. "Ignore me. I'm getting tired, probably guilty of reading too much into things. What say we try and track down Sian and Megan and then call it a day?"

"I think Fiona is right about one thing," James replied a little hesitantly.

"What's that?"

"We're going round and round in circles."

"Yep, there is that, except we do have a very good lead we should check up on. Two, in fact."

"Two? One is Darren Broadstairs, what's the other one?"

"The father. If he lives a few miles away, that would be deemed a commutable distance for a killer, yes?"

James vehemently shook his head. "No way, Ruth! I don't get that at all. Why would he murder Jilly?"

"I don't know," she snapped. "Sorry, I need to look into things more before I can answer that. Don't forget she was his *ex*-wife. I wonder what was cited in their divorce."

"I know that expression. You won't leave any stone unturned until you've discovered the answer, will you?"

"Too right. Why don't you remain here and question the rest of the staff, I think there's only two people now, and I'll go upstairs and interview Sian and Megan?"

"I'd rather we did everything together."

"Why?" she asked, surprised by his statement.

"Safety in numbers, in case we stumble across the killer and he or she doesn't appreciate being tracked down."

Ruth laughed. "Are we talking about my safety or yours here?"

His cheeks coloured up. "Maybe mine," he admitted.

Ruth let out a long sigh. "You really are an idiot at times. As if the killer would do anything stupid like that."

"Who knows? Who would've thought the killer would've targeted Jilly at her own award event party?"

He had a valid point. She leaned over and kissed him. "Do you have enough paper, or shall I get you some more from the receptionist before I leave?"

"I'm fine with this."

She picked up her notebook and tucked it into her jacket pocket. "See you soon. Good luck."

"The same to you. Don't hesitate to give me a shout if you need a hand."

"I won't," she slung over her shoulder as she left the room and walked towards the lift.

"Everything okay?" Maria asked from behind the reception desk.

"Fine. All right if I go up and speak to Miss Lawrence and Miss Drake?"

"Of course. Do you want me to ring them, to make them aware you're on your way up?"

"I'd rather you didn't. The element of surprise and all that." Ruth winked.

The receptionist tapped the side of her nose. "Rooms one hundred and thirteen and one hundred and fifteen."

The lift doors opened, and Ruth stepped in. She waved at the receptionist and waited for the doors to close again. The ascent was a painfully slow one in the antiquated lift. Ruth sensed it was in need of a good service and prayed the thing didn't break down while she was on board.

She let out a relieved sigh when the doors eventually slid open. Ruth marched down the hallway, the butterflies taking flight in her stomach accompanying her on her journey. The first door she reached was room one hundred and thirteen. She tapped lightly. Sian opened the door. She looked an utter mess, mascara streaking down her face. Ruth's heart went out to her.

"Oh, Sian. There's no point in asking how you are, I can see that for myself. Do you mind if I come in for a moment?"

Sian eased herself back behind the door and gestured for Ruth to enter. She noted the suitcase lying on the bed and several of the drawers open. Sian was in the process of packing up.

"Nice to see you again, Ruth. I'm sorry, I'm still an absolute mess."

"That's understandable, you were close to Jilly. Why don't we take a seat?"

Sian sat on the end of the bed while Ruth withdrew the small dressing table stool and perched on that.

"I've barely slept all night. Can't get over what happened. I can't believe she's no longer here to order me around. I know how daft that sounds, but you get used to a certain routine, and it's hard to handle when it gets disrupted."

"I can imagine. What will you do now?"

"I'm going home, back to London. I'll take a week or so off and then start looking for another job. Not the best time to do that, it being the depths of winter, but I'm going to have to. Have you any idea of the cost of living in London? I've only got a one-bedroom flat, and the rent is over fifteen hundred a month. It's daylight robbery."

"That's outrageous. Why live there?"

"Because Jilly was based there. She wanted me to be on hand in case anything cropped up."

"Did she pay towards your rent?"

She leaned forward and plucked a tissue from the box on the dressing table and wiped around her eyes. "You're joking, right? She would never have thought about handing money over for necessities."

"That's terrible. If she expected you to be on hand twenty-four-seven, the least she could've done was pay you properly for the privilege. I hope you received a decent wage from her to compensate."

She shook her head. "I got the going rate. Honestly, I didn't do the job for the money. I did it because I enjoyed it. It gave me a buzz to be on the go all day long. I've never been one for sitting on my backside doing nothing."

"Enjoying your job is one thing, but didn't you ever feel she was taking advantage of you?"

"Not really. Why are you here, Ruth?"

Ruth smiled, admiring the woman's dedication to her tyrannical boss. *You're a better woman than me.* "To see how you're coping, plus I've also been conducting my enquiries with the staff. You're probably unaware of this, but I'm officially investigating the case. The community have come together and raised the funds to prove Steven is innocent."

Sian's eyes immediately widened in surprise. "Really? What do you believe?"

"I think Steven is innocent, too. I've known him for a very long time. He hasn't got a bad bone in his body."

"But Jilly was so angry with him, so dismissive of his obvious talent. Wouldn't that have irked him?"

"I can confirm the way she spoke to him broke him into pieces; however, he enjoyed the event party and had clearly forgotten all about the incident. It was Jilly who invited him to the room last night. I was there when she requested him to join her."

"So he went along and saw the opportunity. Maybe she upset him, and all his earlier rage came rushing back."

"I can understand where you're coming from, but I have to disagree with you. Steven hasn't got a nasty streak. If he had, he would have told Jilly where to stick her demand to replace the set the other day. He didn't. Instead, he rang me, and together we put things right, or that's what we thought at the time. We were both gobsmacked that Jilly hated the second set as well. I have to be honest with you, my blood was boiling on his behalf, but he took it all in his stride. I was tempted to swipe Jilly around the face for the way she spoke to him. He was upset, but as the evening wore on, he accepted her for what she was, a demanding diva, and got on with enjoying himself at her expense."

"I must admit he seems a decent man. All right, if not him, then who do you propose killed her?"

"I have a few suspects on my list of possible killers. The one thing I've yet to determine is a motive. I was wondering if you had anyone in mind."

Her hand flew up to her chest. "Me? Why me?"

"Because you were around her all the time. I'm surmising that Jilly would have confided in you, wouldn't she?"

"Oh, I see. Mostly yes, although she didn't tell me everything. Deep down she was a secretive person, hard to get to the bottom of at times."

"I see. I'd like you to cast your mind back over the last few months. Has there ever been a moment when you felt she overstepped the mark, enough to think her life was in danger?"

Sian frowned. "I don't understand what you're getting at."

"Perhaps she did something underhand to someone. After seeing her reaction to the set debacle, you can't tell me that was a one-off. All I'm asking is if something similar to that incident has happened over the last few months."

Sian placed a thumb and forefinger around her pointed chin, then she chewed on her thumbnail.

"Sian, there is something, isn't there? Please tell me?"

She exhaled a long, loud breath. "There was an incident, as I recall. One of the authors sent me a manuscript to look over—she's a friend of mine. Well, I left it on the desk in Jilly's room. I think she asked me to do something for her, distracted me in some way. It wasn't until the next day that I realised the manuscript was missing. I immediately went back to Jilly's room to ask if she had seen it. She said no. I snooped around the hotel room when Jilly was in the bath and discovered it in Jilly's bedside cabinet. When I tackled her about it, she denied she'd put it there. We had an argument. I told her that my friend had entrusted me with her book and I'd been beside myself believing that the manuscript was lost."

Intrigued, Ruth shuffled forward in her chair. "Why did she hide it from you?"

Sian's head dropped.

"Sian?" she asked when the woman refused to answer.

"I hate saying this, speaking ill of the dead."

"I need to know, Sian, it could be important."

"Well, along with the manuscript, I found an A4 notebook."

"And?" Ruth prompted, her heart racing.

"On the notebook, Jilly had made some notes. She'd obviously read the manuscript and was copying down the basic story."

"No! Really? Why? So she could write a novel and pass it off as her own work?"

"Exactly. I was furious. My friend had sent me that manuscript; she trusted me with it. How on earth could I hand it back and tell her what I thought of it knowing that her story would be recreated by Jilly and probably be a bestseller the day it came out?"

"Does this type of thing happen a lot in the business?"

"Oh yes, every time an author submits a story to a publisher, you can guarantee that story will be rehashed in some way and used nefariously by another author working with that publishing house. Most publishers have ghost writers on hand specifically to take on the jobs. You haven't heard that from me though, okay?"

"It truly is a dog-eat-dog world out there, isn't it?"

"You have no idea what lengths people in this industry are prepared to go to for money."

"It's disgraceful to think publishers are ripping off authors in this way. Isn't there a law against that?"

She shrugged. "There's the plagiarism law, but honestly, you look at any book on the market, you'll find it follows the same formula in a specific genre. It's the different spin the authors put at the end to bring the plot together that sets their story apart in the readers' eyes."

"I suppose I've never really thought about it before. Do you know how many books are written every year and published?"

"It has to be millions. Not only those being published through traditional publishers, but self-published books are causing a right stir within the industry. Some of these authors are making a packet and keeping all the royalties for themselves. 'Proper authors' or trad-published authors earn a pittance in comparison."

"If that's right, then why do authors insist on going after a traditional deal with a big-named publisher?"

"Because of the marketing aspect of things. If publishers think an author is worth backing, they will throw thousands behind them come release day. Independent or self-published authors don't have the funds for that, although I'm aware of quite a few authors out there who are storming up the charts without the backing of a publisher behind them."

"Okay, I get that. It would seem the world of publishing is in the throes of a dramatic change, like everything the world over, nothing different there. So, going back to your friend's manuscript, what happened?"

"I pleaded with Jilly not to do what she intended. We had a major argument that ended with me threatening to expose her."

"Wow! Would you have gone through with your threat?"

Her head dropped again. When she glanced up at Ruth there were bulging fresh tears in her eyes. "Yes. I'm an honest person, Ruth. Things like that don't sit comfortably with me."

"Did you tell your friend?"

"No. I told her that she had a good story and to submit it to a publisher. No doubt that same story will be rehashed and appear under another author's name very soon—it's probably why publishers take months to get back to authors. I was determined that it wouldn't be Jilly Bramley's name on the cover. I wouldn't have been able to live with myself."

"What about the notes Jilly made?"

"I watched her shred them. Felt relieved when the task was over as well."

Ruth ran a hand over her flustered face. "I've gone all hot and bothered, imagining what that author would have gone through if her book had been ripped off by Jilly."

"It's terrible. It's the risk people take putting their work out there. Where there's money to be had in this world, you'll find someone devious enough trying to cash in on things."

"Has anything like this happened before, with Jilly, I mean?"

Sian tutted, and her mouth twisted.

"Oh heck. I take it by your reaction that I've hit on something."

"You have. Last year a similar incident occurred. One of the authors on the circuit actually accused Jilly of plagiarising her book. The whole debate was played out in the media, on the TV news and in every newspaper in the country."

"I don't recall hearing about it. And what was the outcome?"

"The author won substantial damages against Jilly."

"Wow! How the heck did she maintain her reputation and still produce bestsellers?"

Sian shrugged. "Maybe a lot of people missed the case when it was aired on the news, I really don't know. The whole thing was mighty embarrassing for Jilly. She was forced to make a public announcement. The other author accepted her apology, if a little grudgingly."

"Crikey, you don't think she would've taken things further and killed Jilly, do you?"

Sian gasped and covered her mouth. Dropping her hand, she whispered, "That author was at the event. Her name is Sandra Fellows."

Ruth slapped her hand against her forehead and let it slide down her face. "You're kidding me? Is she still here?"

"I don't know. Do you want me to check?"

"If you wouldn't mind?"

Ruth's mind was spinning out of control as she waited for Sian to finish her call.

Sian shook her head. "No. She checked out a few hours ago."

"Oh heck. I don't suppose you happen to know the woman's address?"

"I believe she lives in Devon somewhere. I think it's further south if my memory serves me right."

"Brilliant, hopefully the receptionist will be obliging and give it to me."

"You don't think she could be responsible?"

"Who knows? She has to go down as a possible suspect. Is there anything else you can think of that might help the investigation? I should imagine Jilly would have fallen out with numerous people over the years who would have been tempted to seek revenge."

"I think you might be right, although I can't put a name to any more at this moment, I'm sorry."

"Please don't apologise. If I leave you a card, will you promise to call me if anything comes to mind?"

"Of course. If you promise to keep me informed on how the investigation is going."

Ruth held out her hand for Sian to shake. "That's a deal. Okay, I need to get going, see if I can track Sandra Fellows down by the end of the day."

"Wishing you luck on that one."

Ruth was in two minds whether to call in on Megan Drake or leave it. She fished out her phone and rang James. "It's me, can you talk?"

"I can. I've just interviewed the final member of staff. What's up?"

"I need you to use your charm on the receptionist, see if you can get the address of one of the guests, a Sandra Fellows."

"I doubt she'll give it to me. You know there's a law against hotels divulging that kind of information, right?"

"Data protection, I know. Just try. If not, I have a rough idea where she lives. I'll use another source to get the information I need."

"Okay, I'll try. How long are you going to be?"

"I'm just about to visit the agent now. I should be with you in ten minutes or so, depending on how things go with her. Any news from the staff?"

"I did hear a snippet of news."

Ruth leaned against the wall. "Which was?"

"That one of the waiters brushed past Jake after the murder was announced. He noticed what looked like blood on the bottom of his cream trousers."

"Jake? Maybe he ran into the room to try and save Jilly once he heard, except, I was outside the room, keeping Steven company until the police arrived."

"Now that is odd. Maybe the waiter made a mistake. Perhaps Jake cut himself and didn't notice that it had dripped onto his trousers."

"Yeah, you're right. I'll tell you what I've found out when I see you."

"Tease! That's not fair, I shared my news with you."

"It's too long to go into over the phone. Have patience, dear fiancé." Ruth blew him a kiss and hung up before he could complain further.

She knocked on Megan's door and mulled over the piece of information James had divulged but again discounted it for the time being.

Megan smiled and welcomed her into the room. Again, Ruth noticed the half-packed suitcase on the bed.

"Are you leaving soon?"

"Yes, Sian and I are catching the four o'clock train back to London. What can I do for you, Ruth?"

"I was hoping to have a quick word with you before you leave. Is that possible?"

"Of course. About anything in particular? Dumb question. About Jilly, yes?"

"That's right. Shall we take a seat?"

The room was slightly plusher than Sian's and had two easy chairs with a coffee table off to one side. Sian sat in one of the chairs and Ruth dropped into the other.

"I'm not sure if you're aware or not, but I've been at the hotel all morning conducting interviews with the staff."

"I wasn't aware. How does this concern me?"

"Well, my intention was to speak to Jilly's family and colleagues next. I've already spoken to Sian and Fiona."

"How is Fiona? I keep trying to ring her. Unfortunately, every time I ring, Jake puts the kibosh on me getting through to her. I'm getting the feeling that Fiona isn't handling things very well."

This was news to Ruth. From what she'd seen of Jilly's daughter, she appeared to be handling the situation far better than she would in the same circumstances. "She was down in reception, seeing her father off. She seemed fine to me."

"Lincoln? Was he here?" Megan asked, her cheeks instantly finding some colour.

"Yes, didn't you know?"

"No. That's a shame, I would've liked to have seen him. You know, to have given him my condolences."

"Even though they were no longer married?"

Megan appeared confused by the question. "Just because a couple decide their marriage is no longer working, it doesn't mean they stop caring about each other."

"I suppose. Can you tell me why they got divorced?"

"They simply grew apart. Jilly liked to travel, and Lincoln doesn't. Therefore, Fiona took up the reins of accompanying her around the country to specific events, such as book signings et cetera."

"Even though you and Sian always accompanied Jilly on her travels?"

"We don't accompany her everywhere, at least I don't. Sian tends to be on hand all the time. I have other clients I need to attend to."

"So she was a burden, is that what you're telling me?"

Megan vehemently shook her head. "No, that's not what I was saying at all. You're guilty of twisting my words there, Ruth."

"Sorry. If Fiona accompanied her mother to various locations, does that mean that Jake tagged along as well?"

"No, not in the slightest. He only showed up this weekend because Fiona pleaded with him. She knew how important this event was for Jilly's career and was eager to share the experience with her boyfriend. I think he enjoyed himself, up until the murder occurred, of course."

"I see. What about Lincoln? Did he ever go the extra mile and travel with Jilly?"

"No, he refused to. In the past year Jilly had spent more and more time on the road. That's why their marriage failed."

"Are you saying that the couple still loved each other and it was the distance that caused the marriage to fail?"

"Yes, I suppose I am."

"If he only lives a few miles away, then why didn't he come to the event if they still meant that much to each other?"

"He hated her way of life, did everything to avoid it. There was no way he would've come even if Jilly had dropped him an invitation."

"Okay, I think I understand what you're saying now. I asked Sian this question a moment ago: is there anyone who Jilly has fallen out with recently who you think could've killed her?"

"No, not that I can think of."

"I know she had a volatile nature, I witnessed that myself yesterday. Are you sure she hasn't ticked someone off who could have sought revenge?"

Megan fell silent as she contemplated the question then shook her head. "I can't think of anyone."

"Sian mentioned something about another author attending the event who Jilly had fallen out with. Can you tell me anything about that?"

"Ah, you mean Sandra Fellows. As far as I know, she and Jilly had agreed to put the arguments aside. I think Jilly admitted she was in the wrong and had paid Sandra a handsome fee for the inconvenience, shall we say?"

"Sian didn't tell me that. So there was no remaining animosity between them?"

Megan swept her fringe off her face. "No. If there had been any ill-feelings left between them, I doubt Jilly would have invited her to the event."

"Again, I wasn't aware of that. This is why it's important for me to get different people's opinions on things. It's surprising the nuggets of information you can garner. Over the course of the evening, did you either hear or see anything that you didn't feel comfortable about?"

Puffing out her cheeks, Megan began to shake her head and then paused. "Actually, when I was flying between rooms, I heard several arguments. However, after working with Jilly all these years, there wasn't anything new in that. I would've thought it strange if there was a day or evening when an argument didn't take place. Sian and I were used to that."

"I said virtually the same thing to Sian—you must be angels to have put up with her vile moods and fiery temper. Not sure I would've lasted a day in her employment, not knowing if I had a job to go to the next day after she'd fired me. I hear she did that frequently."

"She did. A daily occurrence at times. You accept it with people in the limelight. They're under a great deal of pressure and tend to take it out on those closest to them."

Ruth nodded and smiled. "It still wouldn't be for me. Did she lash out at Fiona in the same way?"

"Not that I've ever heard. They got on exceptionally well, especially when Fiona insisted on accompanying Jilly around the UK in the past few months."

"What about Jake, did Jilly get on with him?"

"On the whole, I have to say she did. There's bound to be times when the age gap stretches things to the limit. That happens in every relationship, doesn't it?"

"Have they fallen out recently?"

Megan shrugged. "Not that I can remember."

Fearing she was getting nowhere fast with Megan, Ruth decided to wrap the interview up with a final question. "What about you, Megan? Have you fallen out with Jilly lately?"

Megan's gaze drifted to the carpet, and she crossed and uncrossed her legs a few times.

"Megan?"

The agent inhaled a shuddering breath and released it, then said, "If you must know, yes, we fell out recently. I'm not proud of what I did and I will regret my actions until my dying day."

Ruth's interest mounted. "What did you do, Megan?"

Without looking up at Ruth, Megan confessed, "I didn't mean to do it, the temptation got the better of me, and, well, it just happened before I knew what was going on."

"You're not making any sense. Back up and tell me what you did?"

"Jilly had some exquisite pieces of jewellery. There was one piece in particular I absolutely adored. I know it was wrong of me and very foolish, but one day I tried on this rather beautiful sapphire and diamond choker necklace. She entered the room as I was studying it in the mirror and went ballistic. The piece was an anniversary gift from Lincoln that she treasured." Her eyes bulged with tears, and she coughed to clear her throat. "I was mortified she caught me parading around in it."

"What happened?"

She sniffled. "Jilly roughly turned me around and removed the necklace herself. She made a point of digging her nails into my neck in the process. She placed the necklace back in its box, spun me around to face her and glared at me, then, out of the blue she lashed out and struck me around the face several times."

"That must have hurt, not just physically, I mean psychologically, too?"

"It did. The thing is, she thought I was about to steal the damn thing. I tried to reason with her. Insisted that if I'd intended to do that, I wouldn't have hung around trying it on in her suite. I was mortified and riddled with guilt for weeks, no, months after that. If I'm honest with you, I don't think she ever forgave me."

"Are you saying that things were strained between you?"

She sighed and nodded. "Yes. If you must know, I was on the verge of resigning as her agent. I made a pact with myself that I would ensure things ran smoothly for this weekend and then deliver the news once we returned to London."

"Do you think she was aware of your plans?"

"I don't know. Maybe she had an inkling, I'm not altogether sure. There's only a certain amount of walking on eggshells an agent can put up with. I have dozens of demanding clients I need to be there for. Jilly was the one who needed me the most, except she didn't appreciate in the slightest what I truly did for her."

"She took you for granted?"

"Not just me, either. Everyone she came into contact with. She was a demanding individual who expected the best and blew her top when she perceived people didn't deliver the goods, as you and your friend found out."

Ruth nodded.

"Multiply that hatred you saw by a hundred percent, and you'll understand what the rest of us working alongside her had to put up with three hundred and sixty-five days a year. It was demoralising, so draining to live on your wits all the time. I know I shouldn't say this but, in a way, I'm glad she's gone."

Ruth was tempted to gasp at the woman's confession; however, after being on the receiving end of the dead author's temper herself, she completely understood where Megan was coming from. "How far would you have been prepared to go to get her out of your life, Megan?"

Her mouth gaped open. After a moment's silence, she replied, "If you're insinuating that I killed her, you're wrong. Nothing could be further from the truth. I don't have it in me to rob someone of their life."

"That's exactly what I'm saying about my friend, Steven. Sadly, no one was prepared to listen to him when he expressed his innocence."

"Please, you can't tell anyone about what I've said. My career would disintegrate overnight if ever this came out."

"It's okay. I believe you. I doubt I would've done if I'd been investigating the crime with fresh eyes and not aware of how Jilly treated those around her when she was alive. How many other people felt the same way? That's what I need to find out."

"Are you saying you believe the killer is someone who knew her well?"

"Yes, who had been pushed to their limit. Maybe the incident was forced upon them. Just like you had a secret, who's to say that someone else in this hotel didn't also have a secret?"

Megan gasped. "How dreadful. I just don't know who that person could be."

"It's okay. I have a few suspects on my list who I need to speak to. Thanks for what you've shared with me today. Your secret will remain with me."

Relief flooded her features. "Thank God you believe me."

"I'm experienced enough to know what lengths a killer has to be driven to before they commit their fateful act. Yes, Jilly might have ticked you off and humiliated you on occasions, but I doubt you have it in you to exact your revenge by bumping her off."

Megan reached forward and hugged Ruth. "Thank you for believing in me."

"Let's keep this conversation between us, okay?"

The phone rang. Megan smiled and rushed over to the bedside table to answer it. "Hello? On no, what a shame, I really wanted to get back to London today... Okay, thank you for letting me know... Would it be possible to keep the room for another night? Thank you, that's very kind of you." She hung up and collapsed onto the bed. "We're snowed in. They've cancelled all the trains because of the weather."

"Oh heck, that's not good. Do they think it'll be clear by tomorrow?"

"They think so. I suppose I'd better unpack and start rearranging my schedule for the rest of the week. I was due at another book signing in London tomorrow. My client is going to be livid. What's new, eh?" She chuckled.

Ruth walked towards the door. "You'll manage to talk them around. Maybe the signing event will also be postponed because of the weather."

"Good idea. I'll ring them and see. Thanks for listening, Ruth. I hope your investigation leads you to the killer soon."

"So do I. Take care, Megan."

Ruth left the room and decided to walk down the stairs back to the lobby, fearing what would happen if the lift ground to a halt with her inside it. James smiled when she arrived.

"I've had enough for one day. Why don't we set off for home?" Ruth said, linking her arm through his.

"Sounds like a mighty fine idea to me. I'll gather all the paperwork first." He unhooked her arm and rushed into the conference room, emerging a few seconds later with a pile of notes.

Ruth approached the reception desk. "We're going to shoot off now. Will you pass on my gratitude to the manager? He's been most accommodating—you both have."

"You're welcome. I hope you've managed to narrow the suspect list down during your day with us," the cheery receptionist replied.

"I think we've managed to achieve that. See you soon."

James and Ruth compared notes on the way home. By the time they walked through the front door they were covered in snow. Ben bounded up the hallway to greet them.

"Hello, boy. Have you missed us?" Ruth crouched down and hugged him.

He whined in response and licked the snow off her face.

"I'll pop the kettle on," James said, slipping off his coat and hanging it on the coatrack in the hall.

They both removed their shoes and placed them on the doormat, avoiding coming down to a puddle on the floorboards in the morning.

"Sounds like a good idea. I have a few phone calls I want to make before it gets too late."

"I hope one of them is to Gemma. I've been concerned about her during the day."

She placed a hand on his cheek. "It is. You're such a sensitive soul. Hey, I forgot to ask... Did you manage to coerce the address for Sandra Fellows out of the receptionist?"

"Nope, she refused to budge, even when I openly flirted with her."

Ruth swiped his arm. "You didn't? You utter scoundrel. No wonder she gave you the evil eye when we were leaving."

"Did she?" he asked, looking puzzled.

Ruth sniggered. "All right, that might've been me winding you up. That's the last time you help me out on location if that's what you're going to get up to."

He grabbed her and pulled her in for a snuggle. "You know I only have eyes for you, *mon cherie.*"

"Just because you talk a bit of French, don't think you can get around me that easy, buster."

He attempted to kiss her on the lips, but she turned her head to the side and wriggled out of his arms.

"You mentioned something about putting the kettle on. I suggest you do that to make amends for the *faux pas* you've just committed."

He grumbled his way into the kitchen.

Ruth bent down and whispered in Ben's ear, "Don't go getting any ideas, matey. You know which side your bread is buttered, right?"

Ben's head tilted, and he gave her his paw. She kissed it, planted another kiss on his head then stood and walked into the lounge. After grabbing the phone, she stood against the radiator to rid the chill from her bones.

Gemma answered after two rings.

"Hi, how are you?"

"How wonderful to hear from you, Ruth. I'm fine. They've said they're going to discharge me in the morning. I can't wait to get home. I hate hospitals."

"Did they find out what was wrong?"

"At first they thought it was my appendix but later they determined it was food poisoning."

"Ah, we thought that, didn't we? That was quick. It doesn't usually come into effect until hours after you've eaten something dodgy."

"I forgot I ate an egg mayonnaise sandwich at lunchtime. The doctor thought that was the likely candidate as opposed to what I ate at the hotel."

"That would explain the timing then. Ugh, poor you. Where did you buy the sandwich? They should be informed."

"Umm…I made it myself. You know what it's like, the eggs sit in your fridge and you don't have a clue how long they've been in there."

"Smacked wrist. You'll have to write it on the box. Wasn't there a use-by date on it?"

"You're so smart. Of course there was. I never take any notice of the dates. I usually go by wether a product looks or smells off."

"You're gross. Remind me not to accept a dinner invitation from you in the future."

"Charming. I've learned from my mistake now. You'll be safe from this day forward, I promise you."

"I should hope so. I'm glad you're feeling better. I'll catch up with you when you get home, weather permitting."

"What? No visit? No bunch of grapes or beautiful bouquet of flowers?"

"Ordinarily I would, you know that. Have you not got a window on the ward? Look outside. It's a winter wonderland, and driving would be treacherous. I'm with you in spirit. Speak soon."

"Thanks for taking the trouble to check in with me. I appreciate how busy you are. Wait, any news? I heard on the radio that Jilly was found murdered after I left the hotel. I thought I was hearing things. Who did it?"

"I was hoping you wouldn't have heard about that. I was going to tell you everything when you got home. The police have arrested Steven."

"*No! Never!* He'd never ever do a callous thing like that, whether the woman deserved it or not after the way she treated him."

"Which is why I'm investigating the case. Look, why don't you concentrate on getting yourself better, and we'll catch up in a day or two to go over the details? Damn, I've just remembered, it's the Am-Dram club tonight. James and I have only just got home. We've been at the hotel all day questioning the staff as well as Jilly's friends and family."

"What have you gleaned so far?"

James strolled into the room and handed her a mug of steaming coffee.

"We have a few names on our suspect list. I'll probably have to go back there tomorrow to question some folks further. Hey, I've said too much. It wasn't my intention to get you involved in this. Feel better soon. I'll catch up with you in a few days."

"Spoilsport. Okay. Thanks for calling. Send my love to that hunky fiancé of yours."

"I will." Gemma had always had a soft spot for James. Ruth wasn't threatened in the least because Gemma had always been open about the fact. She ended the call and placed the phone back in its docking station. "Gemma sends you her love."

James' cheeks flared up. "Give it a rest, woman. How is she?"

"It was food poisoning. She ate a dodgy sandwich at lunchtime, nothing to do with the food they laid on at the hotel. She's coming out tomorrow."

"That's a relief all round. Glad it was nothing too serious, although that was bad enough. I had it once. Vomited so much I destroyed the lining of my stomach and was on liquids for a whole month. I wouldn't recommend that to anyone who loves food as much as me, I can assure you."

"Ouch! I bet that was torture."

"Kind of. Right, what's next on the agenda?"

"I suddenly realised that I've agreed to meet up with the group tonight. Not sure I'm up to that now, so I'd better ring round and cancel it."

"Want me to help?"

"You're a gem. I doubt they'll be disappointed given the weather."

They spent the next five minutes ringing around the Am-Dram members, and Ruth felt relieved when everyone agreed it would be for the best to postpone the meeting. She rearranged the meet-up to take place on Wednesday at seven instead, if the weather was better by then. If not, they would reassess the situation and go from there. They were all still concerned about Steven and asked her to send on their best wishes when she spoke to him.

"I have one more important call to make and then I'll crack on with dinner," Ruth said, finally feeling warm enough to move away from the radiator and take a seat on the couch next to James.

He patted her on the thigh and kissed the top of her head.

"What was that for?"

"For being you. For never giving up in the face of adversity. You do what you have to do, I'll cook dinner tonight. I think there's a curry in the freezer I can defrost, if that's all right with you?"

"Sounds just what the doctor ordered to keep the cold at bay. I shouldn't be too long."

"There's no rush." He strode out of the room and left her smiling after him.

She was lucky to have him in her life. He wasn't like other men— never demanded too much of her time, always willing to share in the chores around the house. A true godsend. Shame ran through her for taking him for granted for so long and keeping him at arm's length when he'd been so desperate to get engaged.

She almost jumped out of her skin when the phone rang in her hand. She answered it before it rang a second time. "Hello, Ruth speaking."

"Hey, Ruth, it's Louise. How's it diddling?"

"Wow, that's spooky! I was about to ring you."

"Sounds ominous. Why?"

"You first."

"I heard you're investigating the murder at the hotel and wondered if you'd discovered anything as yet."

"Plenty. Lots to go on, a few suspects on the list, but with that comes a lot of frustration."

"How come?"

"I didn't manage to speak to two very important people at the hotel today. One is a waiter who'd rung in sick, and the other was another author who had already left the hotel."

"Any reason why you want to speak to them?" Louise asked tentatively.

"Cheeky! I have my reasons."

"You can be such a pain in the rear at times. The amount of information I share with you when I needn't is nobody's business. Give me a break and tell me."

"All right. I admit you have a valid point. I learned that the author once accused Jilly of plagiarising one of her books."

"Whoa! Get out of here! Why was she at the hotel?"

"Apparently, they had since put any animosity between them aside. The author turned up to lend Jilly support."

Louise whistled. "And you believe that?"

"Not entirely. I'd still like to question her if at all possible."

"And what about the waiter? Did she forget to tip him?" Louise laughed.

"No, again, it's only hearsay I'm working with here, but word has it that the man had a crush on Jilly."

"Crikey, there seems to be a lot of that going around at the moment, what with Mike being somewhat besotted with her."

"Which brings the conversation around to why I was about to call you. I'm aware that Mike was eager to get Jilly's autograph on his books. Did he achieve that on Saturday, even though Jilly refused to do it?"

"He did."

"Why am I not liking the way you said that?"

Louise exhaled a long breath. "Something happened. I don't know what, but something definitely wasn't right when he returned to the table."

"In what respect?"

"I can't tell you."

"You think I should have a word with him? Face to face?"

"I think it might be in your best interest. He can be a cagey so-and-so at the best of times."

"Shall I come and see him at the paper in the morning? The weather's getting worse out there, otherwise I'd nip round to see him tonight."

"I would leave it until the morning. Maybe ring me at work, see if he shows up. He lives out in the sticks and could possibly get snowed in."

"Okay. I'll ring you first thing, and we'll go from there then. What's your gut telling you? Could he be involved in the murder?"

"Wow, that's one question I was not expecting you to ask. I've known Mike for a few years now. While I'd say he has a fiery temper —I should know, I've been on the end of it several times—I don't think he has it in him to hurt someone, let alone kill them."

Ruth tutted. "That's what I'm hearing about everyone involved. God, I'm even guilty of saying it myself about Steven. The truth is, someone hated Jilly enough to stick the knife in, literally."

"I hear you."

"The tough part is finding out who that person is."

"You said you had a suspect list on the go. Do you want to run that past me?"

"Apart from the two I've already mentioned, I had to place Steven on the list, too. It breaks my heart to do it."

"Rightly so, after the way he was treated by Jilly. That must have hurt."

"But he's such a decent guy. He accepted her chastising him. I was the one who got in her face and was angry on his behalf. Does that mean I should put myself on the suspect list? Because I damn well know as much as I was tempted to smack her one, I would never go as far as ending someone's life."

"Sounds like a tough investigation. I don't envy you in the slightest."

"It definitely hasn't been an easy process so far. All right, it's been a long day, and I'm in dire need of sustenance. I'll see you first thing, weather permitting. Thanks for checking in, Louise."

"You're welcome. Enjoy the rest of your evening."

She ended the call and strolled into the kitchen. The aroma of the curry bubbling on the stove wafted through the house, and her stomach rumbled. "That was an exceptional idea of yours to cook up a batch of it a few weeks ago," she praised James.

"I have my uses."

Ruth walked up behind him, placed her arms around his waist and rested her head on his back. "You certainly do."

"Did I hear the phone ring?"

"Yes, it was Louise. It saved me calling her. I've arranged to visit the paper in the morning."

He twisted around, eased his arms either side of her waist and glanced down at her. "Any reason why?"

"I want to have a word with Louise's boss. She hinted that all wasn't well with him on Saturday after he'd asked Jilly to sign his books. I'm intrigued to know what went on."

"As you should be. Sounds a bit off. Okay, I've had enough discussing the case today. Why don't we eat our dinner in front of the television during a film?"

"Sounds like an excellent idea. Rom-com or action movie?" she asked, giving him the option after spending his day off working alongside her.

"Action movie?"

"Fine by me. How long before dinner?"

"Five minutes. Why?"

"I was going to take Ben for a quick snowball fight in the back garden."

"Now I'm jealous."

She kissed him and ran into the hallway to collect her coat and boots. When she returned, she found a panting Ben standing at the back door. "Who said dogs don't understand?" She laughed and ruffled his head.

She formed and threw snowball after snowball until Ben was exhausted.

"Dinner's ready," James shouted from the kitchen.

"Last one for the evening. I promise we'll have another game tomorrow, munchkin."

Ruth dried Ben rigorously with a towel on the back doorstep then let him into the house. The phone rang in the lounge, so she tore off her shoes and rushed through the house to answer it. "Hello," she said breathlessly.

"Oh my. I haven't interrupted anything, have I?" her mother's shocked voice asked.

"No, Mother, you haven't. I was having a snowball fight in the garden with Ben if you must know."

"Thank goodness. How are you, dear?" Her mother sounded rough still.

"We're both fine. How are you and Dad doing?"

"So-so. Your father is a lot worse than me. I fear we're going to have to postpone the trip to Scotland we were planning for the spring."

"Oh no. Do you want me to pop round?"

"There's no need. It's vile out there. No point in you coming over here picking up our germs," her mother stated, ending her sentence with a rasping cough. "Any idea how Carolyn, Keith and the boys are?"

Ruth cringed and squeezed her eyes shut. "Okay as far as I'm aware, Mum."

"I'll give them a ring. Carolyn and I had arranged to go shopping during the week. I fear I'll have to cancel that now."

"Maybe it would be for the best to postpone until you're feeling better. I'm sure she'll understand." Ruth flopped into the couch. "It's been a hectic few days. Have you heard the news?"

"What news? I don't even know what day it is. This cold has knocked the stuffing out of me. Oh my, how did the event go?"

Ruth debated whether to tell her mother about Steven and the murder or not. In the end, she decided she had to for a quiet life. If her mother ever found out that she'd kept her out of the loop on the Carmel Cove gossip, she'd never be likely speak to her again. "Are you sitting comfortably?"

"Yes, I'm on the sofa wrapped up in the quilt. Whatever is the matter?"

Ruth briefly summarised the events of the past few days to the sound of large gasps coming from her mother's end. When she'd finished, her mother remained silent for a long time, processing what Ruth had told her.

"Well, I don't know what to say. Poor Steven. He couldn't possibly have committed the crime, could he?"

"I'm doing my best to ensure he doesn't go down for it. I have to say, though, it's not looking good for him. He's sitting in a cell at the station, awaiting to be transferred to a remand centre. The she-devil inspector has arrested him, only because he was covered in Jilly Bramley's blood. I'm surprised I didn't get arrested as an accomplice—I was standing next to him when the inspector and her boys in blue showed up. My take on it is, if Steven had committed the crime he would have bolted. It would have been totally idiotic of him to remain outside the room, waiting for the police to show up. You try telling the inspector that, though. She's such an imbecile at times."

"That's shocking to condemn a man for caring about a victim. I'm with you on that one. It seems illogical for Steven to still be yards from where the murder was committed. Who's paying you? You can't keep taking on cases that you don't get paid for, love."

"I know. I'm sure the club will arrange a fundraiser of sorts. I'm not doing this for the money, Mum. All I want is for Steven to be proved innocent and set free."

"How's he coping with being locked up?"

Ruth bashed her fist against her thigh for not chasing that up during the day. "I'm going to ring the station after we've had dinner. James and I haven't stopped all day in our quest to clear his name."

"It must be difficult for you, not knowing which way to turn. Okay, I'm going to leave you to have a rest this evening. Sounds like you deserve to put your feet up. Before I go, did you get your boiler fixed?"

"Thankfully, yes, on Saturday. Good job, too, what with the snow coming down."

James entered the room carrying two dishes.

"Here's my dinner now. I'll keep you informed about Steven, Mum. Give my love to Dad."

"He sends his love back to you and James. Speak soon. Don't go worrying about us, your father and I will be fine. Do your best to clear Steven's name."

"Take care, Mum. Love you lots."

"Goodbye, love."

"Oh, before you hang up. We've got engaged." Ruth held the phone away from her ear as her mother's screech rippled down the line, followed by another bout of coughing.

"Well, it's about time. Goody, I'll have a wedding to arrange when I feel better."

Ruth rolled her eyes. James sniggered beside her—he had his head leaning against hers, listening to the conversation.

"We're going to have a small wedding, Mum. Nothing too fancy."

"I'm not liking the sound of that. Your father and I have some money set aside for a big affair."

"You know I'd rather you spent the money on yourselves and enjoyed your travels."

"We can do that as well. We'll discuss it soon. Congratulations to you both. I had a feeling you'd see sense eventually."

"Goodbye, Mum. Speak soon." She ended the call with a large sigh. "Did I do the right thing telling her while she's ill? I hope she doesn't spend the next few days ringing me about this and that to do with the wedding."

James raised an eyebrow. "And when is the wedding likely to be?"

Ruth lifted her fork and slipped a mouthful of curry in her mouth. He nudged her for an answer.

She pointed at her mouth and exaggerated a chewing motion.

He groaned. "I know, it's rude to speak with your mouth full. You can be so infuriating at times, Ruth Morgan!"

9

*M*iracle of miracles, the sun was shining when Ruth woke up the next morning, even though the temperature still felt incredibly low.

Ben was lying on the bed beside her. He'd taken James' place when he'd set off for work at six. She sat up and noticed a note on his pillow.

I **love you, Ruth. Please, please can we get married in the summer? This is the last time I'm going to mention it. The ball is in your court, as usual. I wanted to let you know how much you mean to me and how desperate I am to have you as my wife.**

*U*nexpected tears misted her vision. He was such a caring man, with a romantic streak running through him that she'd never experienced in any of her other relationships. She had a lot of soul-searching to do before she gave him the answer he was seeking. *The note has definitely swung the vote in his favour, though.*

She lavishly stretched and pulled Ben into a cuddle. "What do you reckon, boy? Fancy being a guest of honour at a summer wedding?"

He rolled over onto his back, his legs stretched up in the air, and moaned. She kissed his head then threw the quilt over him. He ended up struggling and wrapping himself up in the heavy quilt. Ruth laughed. It seemed ages ago since she'd laughed so hard. There had been far too much trauma in her life the past few months.

She sprinted into the bathroom, ran the shower to get it steaming hot and fiddled with the thermostat on the radiator, ensuring the warmth of the room hit her as soon as she stepped out of the shower.

After drying her hair and applying the faintest touch of makeup, she rang Louise. Her friend gave her the go-ahead to visit the paper. She set off a few minutes later and fulfilled her promise to Ben to stop at the park en route and call in at the baker's for a sausage roll to share.

She let him run around chasing the squirrels for ten minutes then wiped off the excess snow from his paws before securing him in the back seat. She then trotted down the road to the baker's. The smell was very enticing. She was tempted to buy more than the sausage roll she had gone in for. Instead, she resisted the temptation and handed over the money. Back in the car, she shared the roll with Ben. He could skip his diet for a day. Downing the cup of coffee she'd bought, she then made her way over to the newspaper.

She arrived fifteen minutes later, avoiding the patches of ice here and there in the road. "I'll be back soon, Ben." She left the window down a couple of inches and locked the car.

He barked a few times, letting his annoyance show, but his racket died down by the time she reached the top step leading into the large building that dated back to the eighteen hundreds. Ruth had always admired the architecture of the building from afar and was awestruck when she entered it.

The receptionist smiled. "Hello and welcome. What can I do for you today?" she asked cheerily.

"Nice not to combat the snow today," Ruth replied, returning the smile. "I'm here to see Louise Watson. I have a meeting with her this morning."

"Vile weather, I agree. Ah, yes, Louise mentioned you would be dropping by. I'll get you to sign in and give you a pass—that should prevent nosy reporters from asking who you are and what your intentions are."

Ruth laughed. "Thanks. It's on the fifth floor, isn't it?"

The receptionist was efficient and within seconds handed Ruth her pass and turned the register around for her to sign. "It is. The lift is over to your left. Have a good day."

"Thanks. You, too."

The lift was made of glass and ascended the outside of the building. The views were phenomenal, a winter wonderland with the odd patch of road that had been successfully gritted.

She exited the lift and pushed through the door on her left. An excited buzz filled the room. Someone called her name. She searched around and spotted Louise's hand raised at the very end. Striding through the compartmentalised area, she eventually reached Louise's desk. They hugged.

Louise invited her to take a seat beside her. "You made it then. Isn't it dreadful out there?"

"Hopefully, the sun will melt the snow within a day or two. It's nice to see it now and again, but the novelty wears off quickly, doesn't it?"

"I agree."

"Has Mike arrived?"

Louise motioned behind her with her head. "He's in his office."

Something about the way Louise was acting alerted Ruth to something being wrong. "Does he know I'm coming?"

"It might have slipped my mind to tell him."

Ruth chuckled. "You're almost as devious as me. Do you think he'll see me?"

"He'd look an idiot if he turned you away. Do you want me to announce you're here?"

"It would be good to get it over and done with, not that I'm nervous or anything. You've played me, Louise, I'm not going to forget that in a hurry." She wagged a finger at the journalist who had been a friend and valuable source of information since starting up her business.

Louise sniggered and leapt out of her chair. She knocked on Mike's office door and entered when he bellowed.

Ruth strained her neck to listen. It was obvious Mike wasn't happy when he heard about her arrival. Louise did her best to turn his mood around and encourage him to speak with Ruth. Finally, he agreed, and Louise beckoned her into his inner sanctum.

Her legs almost buckled beneath her when she stood and walked towards his office. *Get a grip, girl. He's hardly going to tear me to shreds, or will he?*

"Pray tell me what the infamous Carmel Cove private investigator wants a word with me about?"

Ruth opened her mouth to speak, but his raised hand silenced her.

"Wait, come in and take a seat. Do you want a coffee? We must get our priorities right."

Ruth swallowed and sat opposite him. "That would be lovely, thank you."

"I'll leave that in your capable hands, Louise."

The journalist left the room and closed the door behind her. Ruth extracted her notebook from her coat pocket and flipped it open. With a pen, she wrote Mike Jones' name at the top of a clean sheet.

"Right. I see you're a woman after my own heart and not willing to hang around. What is it you want to know, Miss Morgan?"

"You can call me Ruth, Mike." He gestured for her to get on with it. He was bolshier than when she'd met him on Saturday night. "When you went to the event on Saturday, the last I heard was that you wanted Jilly Bramley to sign your books for you."

"That's right, and she did, if a little reluctantly. I must say, I'd been looking forward to meeting the author for some time and jumped at the chance to buy a ticket for the evening the second I learned she was coming to town. What a mistake that was," he said, bitterness creeping into his tone.

Ruth glanced up from her notes. "Oh, why?"

The door opened, and Louise entered with the coffees. Mike

nodded his thanks and shooed her out with his hand. It wasn't until Louise had left the room that he answered her question.

"She was evil. Yes, she appeared friendly enough while she was at the event, accepting the awards bestowed upon her, but get her alone, and she was…well, evil. Unable to smile at her devoted fans—yes, I did indeed class myself as a devoted fan, Lord knows why. She treated me abominably. Grudgingly signed my books." He left his desk and removed three books from the shelf behind him. He opened the cover of each of the hardbacks and pointed. "Look, nothing! Only her damn signature." He returned to the shelf and collected another three books, one from Lee Childs, another from Mark Billingham, and the final one was by Stephen Leather. Each of them had written something more than just adding their signature. A vast contrast to how Jilly treated her fans. "See. These three made an effort, she didn't. What a woman. My feelings instantly changed towards her."

"They did. I have to say, I'm not surprised by your admission. I've always been a fan of hers and have felt the same after the way she treated Steven."

"Louise told me about your friend. Do you think he killed her?"

"No," she replied adamantly. "Not for a second. But someone did." Her gaze held his for a moment.

He narrowed his eyes and shook his head. "No way! You don't think I could do such a dreadful thing, do you?"

"I didn't say that. The main reason I'm here is to ask if you saw anything around the time you got your books signed."

"Anything? Do you want to be more specific?"

"It was after the awards ceremony, right? And before she was murdered, yes?"

He nodded at both questions.

"Well, I'm trying to fathom out what went on between those times. Someone, somewhere must have seen something."

"All I can tell you is that I left the banqueting hall and tracked her down to a room just outside, across the hallway."

"Did you see anyone else either in the hallway or in the room with Jilly?"

"No one in the hallway; however, there was a young man in the room, standing behind Jilly while she signed my books."

"A young man? A waiter perhaps?"

"No, sorry, I should've been more accurate. It was the man sitting at the top table with Jilly during the award ceremony."

Ruth raised her head to look at him. "Jake Baker?"

He shrugged. "If you say so. Who is he?"

"He's the boyfriend of Jilly's daughter, Fiona."

"Ah right. If I didn't know any better, I would've put him down as some form of bodyguard, the way he was standing behind her, giving me a death stare. Oops, an admittedly bad choice of words there, sorry."

She waved the comment away. "So he was standoffish, would you say?"

"That's one word for it. Hard to know how to explain his stance and attitude really. I was only in the room a couple of minutes. When I came out, I shuddered. It was as if the atmosphere in the room was exceedingly hostile and frosty."

"That's interesting. I know I'm asking a lot, but would you say that Jilly and Jake had been arguing?"

He flung his arms up in the air, gathered all the books he'd laid out on the desk and returned them to the bookshelf. "I wouldn't like to say. There was something odd about the situation, let's say that."

"Interesting," Ruth repeated. She blew on her coffee and took a sip.

"Who do you think is responsible? Can we get an exclusive with you after you've solved the case?"

"If I solve it you mean."

"According to Louise you're like the proverbial dog with a bone. I have no doubt you'll do it. What's happening regarding your friend?"

"Thanks for your confidence in me. As for Steven, I'm not sure. I need to check up on him today. My guess is he'll be shipped out to a remand centre soon."

"Unless you do your job in the meantime and bring the true culprit out into the open."

"Yes, there is that. I'm going to drink this and get on my way. All right if I have another word with Louise before I leave?"

"Go for it. Keep me informed if you will?"

"I will. I appreciate you taking time out of your busy day to speak to me."

"Always happy to help."

Ruth rose from her seat and left the room. Cup in hand, she approached Louise's desk. "It's all right, you don't have to pretend to be working. I cleared it with him to have another word with you."

Louise relaxed back in her chair.

Ruth sat opposite her.

"How did it go?" Louise asked.

"He told me something that could prove valuable to the case. I can't tell you more than that right now."

"Shame on you for keeping me in the dark. Maybe I'll have to reconsider the type of information I hand over to you in the future."

"Grumpy git! All right. He said that Jake Baker was in the room when the signings took place."

"Who's he?"

"Jilly's daughter's boyfriend."

"And that's significant, why?"

Ruth rolled her eyes. "According to Mike, there was a frosty atmosphere in the room. I probed further. He didn't think it was only because he was there, but he wasn't too sure about that."

"Mike was pretty narked when he rejoined me at the table. He refused to tell me why, though."

"Jilly treated him badly. Signed his books but neglected to put a dedication in them, unlike some other well-known authors he's come across."

"Ouch! That would be pretty tough for a fan to take."

"It would. I'm not going to add him to my suspect list, though."

Louise leaned in and whispered, "Are you putting it down to a wounded ego?"

Ruth wanted to laugh so hard at that comment but suppressed it when she saw Mike watching them with interest through the glass panel.

"I can't respond, he's watching me."

"Oh dear. What's next?"

"I need to stop off at the hotel. See if I can have a chat with the waiter who didn't show up for work yesterday, and then I think I'm going to try and wangle a visit to see Steven. I might have to take his solicitor along with me."

"Good idea. Send him my best wishes. I think it's deplorable that the inspector arrested him the way she did. What's she doing? Have you seen her?"

"Nope. James and I were at the hotel all day yesterday and didn't lay eyes on her. It's beyond me how that woman is still in her job. I'm busting a gut to prove someone's innocence, and she's sitting back accepting that Steven is guilty. I'm devastated for him."

Louise placed a hand over hers. "Don't get upset. I have faith in your abilities to put things right."

Ruth smiled. "Thanks. I wish I had the same confidence in myself. Right, I'd better crack on. Thanks for the coffee. I'll be in touch soon if anything comes to light."

"Take care, Ruth. Be kind to yourself. Not everyone would go the extra mile like you do."

"That means a lot, Louise. See you soon."

They hugged and patted each other on the back.

Ruth left the press room and jumped in the lift once more. As she exited the building, she had her phone in her hand and dialled a number.

"Duggan and Partners. How may I help you?"

"Hi, it's Ruth Morgan. Is it possible to have a quick chat with Wayne, please?"

"Hold the line, Miss Morgan, I'll check if he's available. The client he was seeing has just left, so I think you'll be in luck."

"Thanks so much."

Ruth waited patiently, stamping her feet on the top step to keep them warm.

"Hi, Ruth. What can I do for you?"

"Hi, Wayne, I was hoping you could make a call to the cop shop and make them grant me a visiting order to see Steven."

"Hmm…do you want to wait on the line while I make the call?"

"That would be fab." Mozart filled her ear. It wasn't long before Wayne's voice replaced the peaceful music.

"I'm back. I've secured a slot to see him at noon. Does that fit in with you?"

"Wow, you're amazing."

"I know. I'll meet you at the station."

"You're coming as well?"

"They wouldn't let in any Tom, Dick or Harry off the street to see an arrested criminal, you know."

"I wish you wouldn't call him that."

"Whether you like it or not, Ruth, it's a fact."

"All right, I hear you. I look forward to seeing you at the station. I'll get there early for a change."

"Yes, you're not the best timekeeper in the world, I seem to remember. Don't go bringing him anything. It'll only get confiscated."

"Damn, you read my mind. I was going to pick him up some of his favourite shortbread."

"It would be a waste of time and money. I'll see you around eleven fifty-five."

"I'll be there. Thanks, Wayne."

"My pleasure. Toodle-pip."

She ended the call with a laugh and glanced up the road to the hotel in the distance. A quick stop off at the park to give Ben a bit of exercise, and then she'd head over to the hotel again.

Ben whimpered when he saw her approach the car.

"There, I wasn't long, was I? All that noise for nothing." She plucked a treat from the glove box and handed it to him. He gulped it down and then licked her hand, looking for more.

She drove to the park and watched him run towards his poodle friend whose owner was standing nearby. "Hello, Cynthia, how's it going with the renovations?"

"Mustn't complain, although I'm going to about this damn weather. We're cold enough as it is up there at present without having to contend with these plummeting temperatures."

Ruth rubbed her gloved hands together. "I thought it would be warmer today, what with the sun shining. But I think it's colder than yesterday, if that's possible."

"I believe you're right. Your sister and brother-in-law have been super helpful. Thanks for putting me in touch with them, Ruth."

"I'm so glad to hear that. It's always tough moving to a new area and getting your bearings. A guiding hand from locals is always a great help. So many people get ripped off these days. It's great when that can be avoided, and you source the traders you can trust."

"I know, that's so true. I once took my car in for a service to a new garage I'd stumbled across. I was expecting a service bill of around one hundred and fifty, and they charged me a staggering three hundred and eighty pounds. Disgraceful behaviour."

"How awful. What did you do about it?"

"I reported them to Trading Standards and the Citizens Advice Bureau. They advised me to claim the excess back from the garage. Of course, the garage refused. I was determined not to let them get one over on me and ended up taking them to the small claims court."

"Go you. I have to say, I would've done the same. How did you get on?"

"I ended up paying the one-fifty I was anticipating paying. The garage owner was livid. The judge said that too many women get ripped off by businesses nowadays."

"I'm inclined to agree with them. Whenever I book something in, like my car, I always give my name as Mrs Morgan. It seems to do the trick."

"What a world we live in. Anyway, how are things with you? How's that friend of yours doing, you know, the one whose husband was murdered?"

"She's coping well from what I gather. I need to check in on her soon. I've been snowed under, excuse the pun, with another investigation."

"Oh, which one?"

"You must've heard about the murder at the hotel on Saturday?"

"I did. No, you're investigating that? Why?"

"My dear friend, Steven Swanson, has been accused of the murder."

Her hand flew up and covered the side of her face. "No. Did he do it?"

"No. I don't believe so. He was a huge admirer of the author who was killed. But the fact he was found covered in her blood doesn't bode well for him in the eyes of the law."

"Golly, why would he touch her if he didn't do it?"

"He was trying to revive her. I think I would've done the same, wouldn't you?"

"It's hard to say, dear. Perhaps I might've felt for a pulse, avoiding any bloody parts. Covered in her blood? Sounds a little suspect to an outsider."

"I know how it sounds, believe me. I'm going to do all I can to make sure the truth comes out. Right, I have to be somewhere at twelve and I have another visit to make before then. It was lovely chatting with you again. Take care on the icy pavements."

"I will, dear. Good luck with your investigation."

"Ben, come on, boy. Stop your flirting now, we have work to do."

When they got back to the car, she wiped the excess snow off Ben and buckled him into his harness then headed over to the hotel.

Maria smiled. "Hi, how's it going?"

Ruth's mouth turned down at the sides. "I think I'm getting some-where, just need to question a few more people. Talking of which, Darren Broadstairs wasn't available for me to interview yesterday. I don't suppose he's shown up for work today, has he?"

"You're in luck, he started about half an hour ago. Do you want me to see if he's free for a chat?"

"That would be great—if you're sure I won't be disrupting his work?"

"I don't think so. I'll check with Mr Strong first." She disappeared into the office behind the reception desk and emerged a few seconds later. "You're free to speak with him. Why don't you sit over there? I'll order a coffee for you and insist on Darren serving you."

"Excellent. Thanks so much." She moved away from the desk and sat in the foyer, jotting down a few notes ready for when Darren showed up.

Five minutes later, a lanky young man with acne-covered skin deposited a tray on the table. "Hello, there. Here's your coffee. The boss said you wanted a word with me?"

"That's right." She held out her hand. "You must be Darren. I'm Ruth Morgan, the local private investigator. Take a seat."

His eyes widened, and he lowered himself into the rounded chair opposite her. "Seriously? I've never met a PI before. You're definitely not how I expected one to look."

Ruth smiled as her cheeks heated up. "Thank you, I'll take that as a compliment. I wanted to ask you about the murder that happened here on Saturday. You were on duty that night, is that right?"

"I was. It was terrible. I've always loved reading her thrillers. I bet she never dreamed she'd end up like a victim from one of her books."

"You enjoyed her books?"

"Yes, I am, sorry, *was* a huge fan."

"Did you get a chance to speak to Jilly Bramley when she was alive?"

"Of course. Well, not speak-speak…I served her breakfast and dinner while she was here. I would never dream of crossing the boundaries."

"Fraternising with the guests is deemed as crossing the boundaries, I take it?"

"That's right. We get quite a few celebrities staying here from time to time. We're expected to treat them like all our other guests and keep a distance. It works most of the time until someone as famous as Jilly Bramley walks through the door."

"You were eager to speak to her then? What with you being a huge fan and all?"

"Yes. The trouble is, she showed up at the beginning of last week, and my shifts didn't start until the end of the week. By then, she was caught up with ensuring the event ran smoothly. I tried on several occasions to have a brief chat with her but didn't have much luck. She constantly waved me away, insinuating I was pestering her. I swear I wasn't. There are some people in this life who intrigue you more than others. She was one of those people."

"Intrigued by her as a person or by the stories she told?" Ruth asked, taking a sip of her coffee.

"A bit of both, I guess. I have been known to pen short stories in my spare time. It's my ambition to obtain a publishing deal for a novel one day."

"Interesting. What genre do you write?"

"Thrillers, mainly, maybe a touch of adventure thrown into the mix, too. What with Jilly writing a number of bestselling thriller novels, I was hoping she would've had some spare time to chat with me. I guess dozens of wannabe authors asked her the same boring questions over and over. I tried to be imaginative when I got the chance. She looked at me as if I had no right to breathe the same air as her, let alone anything else."

"That must've come as a shock? To build yourself up like that, eager to seek advice, only to be shot down in flames?"

He sighed and picked at a bit of fluff on his trousers. "I have to admit, it hurt. I always thought she was a nice lady, but when you met her in the flesh, well…she wasn't as nice after all. Everyone seemed to be on tenterhooks around her. Afraid to speak or have an opinion for themselves. At least, that's the way it came across to me. My hopes were dashed the moment I was privy to what she was like in real life. Do you think it was the fame that changed her?"

Ruth shrugged. "I'm not sure. I didn't really know the lady. Yes, I was a huge fan, but I have no idea what she was like in real life. Sometimes famous people put on a show for the general public."

"You're saying they're two-faced?"

"Perhaps. Going back to Saturday… Around the time that Jilly was murdered, where were you?"

"I was in and out of the kitchen, ferrying dirty dishes et cetera from the banqueting hall. Mr Strong is hot on that. Hates a room to look untidy and expects us to clear away the dirty dishes immediately after people have eaten."

"I can understand that. While you were clearing the room, did you happen to notice anyone in the hallway?"

His brow furrowed, and he scratched the side of his face as he thought. "I saw Jilly go into the room she was using, you know, the one where she was found murdered."

"Anyone with her at the time?"

"No. Although, on one of my many trips I saw the man who was accompanying her on the visit enter the room as well."

"The young man? Her daughter's boyfriend?"

"Yes. I got the impression he was like a bodyguard to her. He always appeared edgy, glancing over his shoulders as if making sure the coast was clear of fans."

Really? Now that's interesting!

"I don't think he had anything to do with her other than being Fiona's boyfriend. I might be wrong about that, though. I'll need to clarify the situation when I see them next. So, he was in the room with her. Did you see anyone else?"

"I suppose the other two women travelling with her dipped in and out at various times, although that could've been earlier on in the evening. I can't be sure how accurate that is. The murder has thrown me, sorry. I've never known anyone who was killed before. It sends shock waves through your system, I can tell you."

"I appreciate that. You're doing well. Can you recall anyone else entering that room during the evening?"

"There was one other man I seem to remember. He had a bunch of books in his hands. I recognised them as Jilly's. He went into the room the same time I entered the banqueting hall. Once I'd collected a pile of plates, I was just about to leave the hall when he came barging through the door. Almost ended up on my backside, I did. He mumbled an apology, embarrassed by what he'd done. I accepted it and brushed it off. That type of thing happens quite a lot during a function, especially when guests have had a drink or two."

Ruth knew exactly who Darren was talking about, Mike. As she'd already discounted him from her enquiry, she brushed over it. However, hearing him mention Jake, Sian and Megan got her investigative juices flowing again. "How soon did you see the two women accompanying Jilly and the young man who you thought was her bodyguard before the murder took place? Can you tell me that?"

"I can't narrow it down to specific times. I was super busy. I wish I could. I feel such a failure that I can't give you more information."

"Don't worry."

"Oh wait," he shouted, startling her. "There was another guy I saw. He was leaning against the wall, his hands covered in blood. He was the man the police arrested."

"Yes. My friend. I believe he's innocent. That's why I'm investigating the crime. I'm sure the information you've given me will prove beneficial going forward. I can't thank you enough."

"Is that it? Can I go now?"

"You can. Wait a second, and you can take this with you." She finished what was left of her coffee and placed the cup and saucer back on the tray. "That was lovely, thank you."

"You're welcome. I hope you catch the culprit soon. I have to say I'm surprised the police aren't sniffing around."

Ruth shook her head. "They have a man in custody, there's no need for them to carry on their investigation."

"Crikey, if your friend is innocent, that's a bummer of a situation to find himself in."

"I'll do my best to get him released, don't worry."

"Good luck." Darren took the tray and exited the foyer.

Ruth approached the receptionist once more. "Thanks for allowing me to see him. It was an informative meeting."

"No problem. Anything else we can do for you?"

Ruth glanced at her watch. She had twenty minutes to get to the station. She tutted. "I'd love to hang around and question some of your guests again, but the trouble is, I have a meeting to attend to soon, one I can't get out of."

"That's a shame. Perhaps we'll see you later on."

"Depending how the meeting goes, that's a possibility."

Ruth said cheerio and left the hotel. She drove to the police station and parked in the lot close to Inspector Littlejohn's car. She decided to let Ben out and walked past her car, not caring if Ben cocked his leg up one of the inspector's tyres. In fact, when he didn't, she couldn't help but feel disappointed. Spotting Wayne's Mercedes pulling up, she bundled Ben back in the car, gave him a treat and kissed the top of his head. "I won't be long, I promise."

Ben barked and barked once she locked the car. She glanced around her in all directions, embarrassed by the noise.

Wayne chuckled when he exited his vehicle with his briefcase. "Sounds like your dog is objecting to being left alone. Do you always take him to work?"

"Every day. We usually spend most of our time in the office or driving around on surveillance. I don't leave him alone much. However, when I do, he objects noisily. That's usual for a man, right?"

"Not!" Wayne replied adamantly.

"I have to say, I'm a little apprehensive about going in there."

They proceeded to walk towards the station.

"May I ask why? Are you guilty of something that you'd like to confess to, Ruth?"

"No, I am not! How dare you even think that of me?"

"Lighten up. It was a joke. The only thing you're guilty of, I suspect, is taking life too seriously."

She raised a hand. "Guilty as charged. Especially when my friend's life hangs in the balance."

"Understandable. Come on, put a smile on your face, in spite of the weather. He'll need to see a brighter, less despondent you."

She forced a smile and nodded. "I know you're right. Okay, let's do this."

They entered the old building and announced their arrival to the desk sergeant. He instructed them to take a seat. Ruth sat and watched the sergeant make a phone call. She waited for a constable to appear. However, Inspector Littlejohn filled the doorway instead, her gaze immediately homing in on Ruth. *Damn, that's all I need. Thank goodness Wayne is here with me.*

Littlejohn approached them. "Hello, may I ask what you're doing here?"

Her question was directed at Ruth. She kept quiet, hoping that Wayne would jump in and supply an answer.

"She's with me. We've made arrangements to see my client. Do you have a problem with that, Inspector?"

"I see. Well, this is ordinarily against police procedure, but I'm willing to bend the rules on this occasion."

"I don't think it is, but I accept you being amenable in this instance. Will it be possible to see my client now? Time is money after all."

"I'll arrange it with the desk sergeant. I hope you're behaving yourself, Miss Morgan?"

"I always behave myself, Inspector," Ruth replied, flashing a toothy grin.

The inspector spun on her heel and crossed the room. She and the desk sergeant held a muffled conversation for a moment.

"Interview room one will be open for your use for thirty minutes. Make good use of it. I'll collect Mr Swanson myself. Stay here."

Wayne waited until Littlejohn was out of earshot then said, "She's a nasty piece of work. I've never seen this side of her before. Do you bring out the worst in her?"

"Obviously, if you've never witnessed her vile temper."

"Never mind. Let's set that aside for now. I can hear footsteps."

"Come with me," the inspector shouted from the doorway as she passed by with Steven.

Ruth held back a little to let Wayne go down the hallway first. He motioned with his hand for her to hurry up and walk beside him. Her heart fluttered like a trapped bird trying to escape a confined space. Steven's shoulders were slouched. Even from the back he appeared to be a broken man. All she wanted to do was hug him, reassure him that everything was going to be all right, but she doubted whether either was going to be possible with the inspector in the same room as them. She leaned over and whispered to Wayne, "She won't be here during the interview, will she?"

"I doubt it. No, correct that, I'll make sure she isn't."

"Good."

The four of them entered the room. Steven's handcuffs restricted his movements. Ruth was horrified to see that and noticed a twinkle in the inspector's eye. Ruth hastily looked away.

"Thank you. You can leave us now, Inspector," Wayne said, dismissing the obnoxious detective.

"Thirty minutes. I'll collect him then." She stormed out of the room, slamming the door behind her.

Poor Steven, whose nerves were apparently in tatters, almost jumped out of his skin.

Ruth rushed forward and hugged him. "Oh, Steven. All this must be terrible for you."

Tears cascaded down his cheeks. "It is. Ruth, I'm begging you, you have to get me out of here before I kill myself."

"Don't say that. I'm doing my best, I promise I am."

"Okay, let's sit down. Knock all the angst and the reprisals on the head. Let's discuss this like adults and see if we can come up with a beneficial solution," Wayne suggested, pulling out two chairs for him and Ruth on the other side of the table to Steven. The demoralised man flopped into his chair, placed his cuffed hands on the table and linked his fingers tightly until his knuckles turned white.

"How are they treating you, Steven?" Ruth asked, reaching for his hands.

He withdrew his hands, and tears automatically welled up in her eyes. She'd failed him. He was retreating into himself. She got the impression that she was losing him as a friend.

"How do you think? Like a common criminal. They don't believe me, no matter how many times they bring me in this room to interrogate me. They're trying to force me into writing a confession. I have no intention of doing that."

"You're wise not to do it. Once they have a confession, there will be no going back. We're doing our best for you," Wayne assured him.

"You are? Then tell me, why am I still in here, charged with that odious woman's murder? Why?"

"These things take time, Mr Swanson."

"Please, Steven, I haven't stopped. I spent all day yesterday at the hotel with James, questioning the staff, her family and her friends. Before I came here today, I went back there to interview a member of staff who wasn't at work yesterday. You know I won't let you down."

He sniffled, snot billowing from his nose. Ruth extracted a tissue from her pocket and handed it to him.

"I didn't do it. Why won't they believe me? I found her like that. I'm not saying I wasn't tempted to slap her a few times over the past week or so, but it destroys me that people think I would be capable of taking someone's life."

"Your friends don't think that, Steven."

"They don't count," he replied miserably.

"They do. We're all rooting for you. Please don't give up on us, on me. I'm fighting hard to find the real culprit."

"Thank you. You know they're shipping me out to a remand centre today, don't you?"

"I'd heard it would be soon. There's nothing we can do about that. It would be a different story if the murderer stepped forward and confessed," Wayne said.

Steven snorted. "How likely is that?"

"Not very likely at all," Wayne piped up.

"You say you've questioned everyone at the hotel. What conclusions have you come to, Ruth?"

"I can't really say right now. I have a list of suspects I need to do some background checks on before I can tackle them further. You'll have to trust me. If I go in hard, it's possible that I might scare them off. Patience is going to be the key going forward."

"*Patience*," Steven screeched. "Why are you expecting me to have patience? You're not the one confined to a cell, staring at the white walls for hours on end."

"I'm sorry, it's the best I can do for now, Steven. I'm devastated that you think I'm not doing enough for you. Nothing could be further from the truth, I promise you."

His chin dropped onto his chest. "I'm sorry. I'm beside myself. I don't know what to believe any more. I find myself wondering if I did do it."

"Don't say that, Steven, I know in my heart you didn't kill her. All I need to do now is prove it. I won't give up until I've done that. You need to remain strong. If you keep saying things like that, they'll work on you, play with your mind, try to force a confession out of you. Don't let them win. It's been less than forty-eight hours. Give me a few days more to find the person responsible." She patted his hand and smiled. "If nothing else, you know how much I enjoy rubbing the inspector's nose in it. Have faith, keep the faith in me. I never let my friends down, right?"

"I know. I believe you, Ruth. All I'm doing is urging you to find the culprit quicker. I swear, every time they bring me a knife and fork, I'm tempted to dig one of them into my wrists. I haven't eaten a damn thing since I arrived. I can't, my throat is clogged up with emotion. If I attempted to eat, I'd probably end up choking on the food."

Ruth gasped. Tears dripped onto her cheek as desperation to help Steven took hold. "I'm so sorry. Hang in there, Steven, we'd hate to lose you."

His gaze met hers. "Then get me out of here, because this lot are wrong in their assumption, and I'm the one who is going to take the fall for them screwing up. Please, if you do nothing else in your lifetime, Ruth, you have to help me to clear my name."

Ruth looked at Wayne. His eyes were twinkling with unshed tears as well.

Her gaze drifted back to Steven. "We'll clear your name, I promise you. All we ask is that you start eating properly and hang in there. It might take us a week or two."

He threw himself back in his chair and ran his hand through his hair. "I'll never last. I'm not cut out to be a caged criminal. You don't realise how torturous it is to spend hour after hour confined to a cell, alone with your pitiful thoughts, unable to prove your innocence."

"I can imagine." Ruth turned to Wayne once more. "Isn't there something you can do? Get him bail or plead with them to keep him here for a few more days? I hate the thought of him going somewhere new and being subjected to further turmoil."

"My hands are tied. He's been arrested for murder. In the eyes of the law, murderers are never given bail. All I can do is ask them for leniency in their quest to transfer Steven. I'll have a word with the inspector, try and get on her good side, if she has one."

Ruth felt he'd just dealt her a sucker punch to the gut. "Good luck with that," she mumbled.

"Can't you put your hatred of her aside for a few days, Ruth? For me?" Steven's voice was cracking under the strain.

"I'll do anything for you, you know that. All right, let's see what Wayne can sort out and go from there. I can't emphasise enough how important it is for you to remain positive. You need to start eating, if only to keep your strength up for the fight which lies ahead of you. Promise me you'll do that, Steven? If not, you'll die."

His head dropped, and he nodded. "I'll do it for you, if you'll promise to get me out of here soon."

"Take my word on that. We're going to go now. The sooner I get back on the trail, the sooner you'll be back with us at the Am-Dram club. Everyone sends their love. We're all behind you. Please don't give up."

"I'll do it for you and the group."

His head rose, and for the first time Ruth had something to cling on to as the faintest of smiles appeared on his face.

Just then, the door burst open and the inspector put an end to their meeting. "Your time is up." She walked towards Steven and placed a hand under his elbow, helping him to his feet.

Ruth smiled at her dear friend. "Remember what we said—dig deep, love. See you soon."

"I love you, Ruth, you're the greatest friend a person could have fighting their corner, I realise that now."

"You'd better believe it," Ruth replied, challenging the inspector with a glare.

The four of them left the room again.

"Wait there, I'll be back in a moment. I want a quick word before you both leave," the inspector instructed tersely.

Wayne and Ruth waited anxiously in the reception area, under the gaze of the desk sergeant and a constable carrying out their duties off to the left. Ruth heard the cell door bang and the inspector's heels in the corridor as she made her way towards them.

When she arrived, her gaze fell on Ruth. "I have no idea what you're planning, Miss Morgan, but in my role as senior officer in charge, I'm warning you that you're taking the risk of being arrested yourself if you interfere with this investigation."

Ruth tilted her head. "That's funny, I wasn't aware there was an investigation going on. Correct me if I'm wrong, but you haven't been near the crime scene since Saturday night. I have. Had you questioned the staff, as I have, you would've been told about a few incidents which would probably raise your suspicions along with a nagging doubt whether you have arrested the right man. I can assure you, after digging non-stop for the past thirty-six hours, you have the wrong person in custody."

"If you'd like to come up for air and stop wittering on for a moment, Miss Morgan."

"Sorry. Go on."

"I was about to say I'm willing to listen to any hearsay you've gleaned during your interviews."

"Why should I hand over my hard work, yet again, so that you can take the praise, the way you usually do when we're in a similar situation?"

Wayne held his hand up between them. "Stop. This isn't helping the situation. Inspector, my client has assured me he had nothing to do with the crime, and from what Miss Morgan has told me so far, I also believe that Mr Swanson is innocent. Furthermore, I will be putting in a request either with you or with your superiors not to transfer him to a remand centre. He's struggling as it is. I fear moving him now would finish him off completely. Surely you can see with your own eyes that he's not a hardened criminal, Inspector?"

Her chest inflated as she sucked in a breath. "I'm not admitting anything along those lines, Mr Duggan. What I would be willing to do is sit down and speak with Miss Morgan, run through the information she has gathered so far and look at the situation from a different angle. Are you up for that, Miss Morgan?"

Ruth bit her lip, debating whether she should trust the detective or not.

Wayne nudged her with his elbow. "What do you say, Ruth?"

She shrugged. "It can't hurt. I'll share if you'll reconsider shipping Steven out today."

"I will, if the information proves to be valuable."

"Right. I'll get on with the rest of my day and leave you two to talk like adults," Wayne announced, already heading for the main door.

Ruth's shoulders slumped in resignation when she turned to Inspector Littlejohn and saw the triumphant expression etched on her face.

"Why don't we go upstairs to my office?"

Ruth inwardly groaned. "Why not?"

The inspector swivelled and took off up the stairs. Ruth tagged along behind her. When they walked into the incident room, a shocked James stared at her.

"Get on with your work, Winchester," the inspector ordered. "Through here, Miss Morgan. Would you like a coffee?"

Caught on the hop, Ruth automatically said yes, never one to turn down a cup when it was offered.

"Winchester, two cups of coffee. Make it snappy, we haven't got all day."

Relief swept through Ruth, knowing that the meeting ahead of her was going to be a short one. The inspector sat behind her cluttered desk and gestured for Ruth to sit opposite. There was no small talk between them, which immediately got Ruth's back up.

"Pray tell me what you know about the murder so far, Miss Morgan." There was something about the inspector's condescending attitude that irked Ruth.

"Not much really. What I do know is that Steven didn't commit the murder."

"So you've told me from the outset. What I need is factual

evidence that backs up your claim." Littlejohn picked up a pen and tapped it on the desk.

Each time the pen connected with the desk, Ruth winced. *What an absolute...cow, for want of a better word.*

There was a knock at the door, and an uncomfortable-looking James entered the room. He deposited the coffees on the desk and retreated without uttering a word. *Gosh, I'd hate to work with her all day long. No sign of gratitude.*

"Thank you," Ruth muttered before he left the room. She felt they had reached a stalemate. On the one hand she was desperate to share what she'd learned, if only for Steven's sake; however, her obstinacy was proving to be too much for her to handle. "I've spoken to all the staff at the hotel. They've hinted at certain things that I have no way of proving. I'm in the process of carrying out further checks on a few people on my suspect list."

"Is that it? Why are they suspects?"

Ruth's cheeks flared up. "Mainly due to the hearsay of others."

Littlejohn's mouth twitched into an I-told-you-so smile. "And there lies the problem. In our line of business, we prefer to work with facts, Miss Morgan. And the *fact* remains that Mr Swanson was found at the scene covered in the blood of his victim."

"In the blood of *the* victim. The blood he picked up through no fault of his own when he tried to resuscitate Jilly Bramley. I repeat, not for the first time, do you really think it would have been wise for Steven to hang around at the scene when he was aware the police had been called?"

"Perhaps he realised the game was up when you discovered him."

"That's utterly preposterous."

"Is it? He has the look of a defeated man. Would that be the case if he were innocent? My experience tells me how to judge people when they are arrested. He is showing all the signs of resignation that comes from being caught red-handed."

"Not everyone reacts the same way, surely? I know that from my own experience. Please, won't you reconsider? He's a decent man, a law-abiding citizen who deserves to be treated better."

She remained silent as if mulling over Ruth's plea. "I'll tell you what I'll do... If you share the details of what you've learned so far, I'll promise to reexamine the case, how's that?"

"And take the credit for my hard work again?"

"I can see you're not prepared to work with me on this one, Miss Morgan. I suggest you go about your day and stop wasting your efforts on a friend who will remain guilty in my eyes and the eyes of the law."

Leaving her drink untouched, Ruth rose from her chair and stormed towards the door. She pulled it open and slung over her shoulder, "You'll never change, Inspector. You're too bloody-minded to care about what goes on in this community."

The inspector sat behind her desk with a self-righteous grin. "Good day, Miss Morgan."

Ruth walked out of the office and slammed the door behind her. She marched through the incident room, under the gaze of Littlejohn's team.

"Ruth, what's going on?" James asked under his breath when she was only a few feet away from him.

"She's unbelievable. I have no idea how you put up with her day in, day out. I'll see you at home later."

"Calm down. Drive carefully, it's slippery out there," he called after her.

"Don't worry about me. I have a killer to catch and a friend to prove innocent, in spite of what your boss thinks. Shame on her, and shame on you guys for not standing your ground when you believe someone has been arrested by mistake." Her words were directed at James. She cringed as her mouth ran away with her.

Damn, I didn't mean to take it out on him.

Ruth hugged Ben when she got back to the car. He'd been the only one capable of calming her down when she'd taken her anger out on James in the past. "Come on, let's go for a walk. I need to clear my head."

It was during her walk with Ben that she decided on her next move. It was obvious she was on her own with this one. It was time she put all the information she'd gathered together and did something about it.

10

$\mathcal{W}$ith renewed determination, after walking Ben around the park a few times, Ruth returned to the hotel. In the foyer, she found Fiona and Jake. They appeared to be checking out of the hotel.

With a smile pinned in place, she approached the reception desk. Fiona continued to speak to the receptionist while Jake watched Ruth.

"Are you leaving today?" Ruth asked.

"Yes, the trains are running now. Only on a limited service, but it'll do," Fiona replied.

Jake picked up a couple of the bags and moved them closer to the door, then he returned to collect another two. He had on a pair of cream trousers. Her gaze immediately dropped downwards. A splodge of red marred the hem.

"I was hoping to have a chat with you both before you leave. Over a cup of coffee perhaps?"

Fiona anxiously glanced at Jake. He shook his head. "I'm sorry, Ruth, our train is due to depart for London in twenty minutes."

"That's a shame. Not even a brief chat? It's really Jake I wanted to have a word with actually."

"Say what you've got to say," Jake said, an aggressive undertone to his voice.

"Maybe you'd like to tell me how you ended up with blood on your trousers, Jake?" Ruth pointed at the red blotch on his leg.

The receptionist leaned over her desk and gasped.

Fiona stared at Jake in disbelief. "I hadn't noticed that. Yes, Jake, how did that happen?"

He fidgeted, moving from one foot to the other. "It must've been when I walked into the room and found your mother."

Ruth shook her head slowly. "I don't think so. It was Steven who found Jilly, who tried his hardest to resuscitate her. I came along and found him in the hallway, even went into the room to see for myself what had happened to Jilly. You were nowhere to be seen."

"That's right. You were with me when we received a call from the hotel manager, Jake. What's going on?" Fiona demanded.

He shook his head. "You're wrong, Fi. You're confused. You're grieving. You know your head has been all over the place since you heard the news."

"My brain isn't that fuddled, Jake," Fiona insisted.

Sensing the tension was mounting, Ruth slipped her hand into her pocket and gripped the can of pepper spray she kept in there for emergencies.

Jake's features darkened.

"You see, I've spent the last few days at the hotel, questioning the staff and other guests, and several people reported seeing you go into that room with Jilly. Not only that, but these people also said they heard raised voices. Would you mind telling me what you argued about?"

"Those people are *wrong*. I was upstairs with Fiona, wasn't I, love?"

"No, not all the time. You told me you were there when Mum signed some books for the man from the local newspaper and that you thought Mum treated him appallingly."

"That's correct. I left the room after that."

Ruth could tell his confidence was slipping the more Fiona challenged him.

She moved a few steps closer to Fiona. Jake retreated a little. He glanced over his shoulder at the door.

"Why did you do it, Jake? Were you concerned Jilly was causing a rift between you and Fiona? You hated her travelling with Jilly, didn't you? Were you jealous of their relationship?"

Fiona gasped. "You were, weren't you? The day I told you that she and Dad were getting a divorce, I saw a change in you. When I mentioned that Mum had asked me to travel with her, replacing my father, that's when the arguments started between us. I thought bringing you on this trip would be an eye-opener for you. Make you appreciate why Mum needed someone to be with her, other than Sian and Megan, that is."

Jake sneered and flung his arms up in the air. "You two don't know what you're talking about." He made a grab for Fiona's hand. "We have a train to catch."

Fiona snatched her arm away. "There'll be others. I want this sorted *now*."

He dropped his arm and clenched his fist. Ruth tightened her hand around the pepper spray in her pocket. She spotted the receptionist dip into the room behind her, the manager's office, hopefully seeking help.

"I was desperate to marry you. I went to her to ask for your hand in marriage. She refused, told me I wasn't worthy of you."

Fiona's hand cradled her cheek. "So you killed her?" she asked, horrified.

"She pushed me. I tried to persuade her to change her mind. She was having none of it, so I thought threatening her with my penknife would help."

"What? I can't believe I'm hearing this," Fiona said.

"What happened, Jake?" Ruth asked, keen for him to continue.

He ran a shaking hand through his short hair. "She went crazy, lunged at me when I was least expecting it. The knife pierced her stomach…" His voice faded a little at the end.

Is that remorse?

"What? Why didn't you try to help her?" Fiona asked, her voice faltering.

"I panicked. I knew Swanson was due to turn up, so I jumped out of the window before he could see me in there. I came in that way and went up to the room in the lift. The manager rang us not long after."

"You let someone else take the blame?" Fiona said. "You heartless...I don't know you at all."

"It's not too late, Fiona. I did this for you. I love you. Come away with me. We can go on the run together. We'll have your inheritance to live off."

"Run off with a murderer? Are you *insane*? You honestly think I could love you after you telling me that you're guilty of killing my mother? Geez, you're warped. What makes you think I'd want to breathe the same air as you now? You're sick. Mother's instincts were right about you. She told me numerous times not to trust you. I thought she was being overprotective, but she was right. You're not all there."

Jake's gaze darted between Fiona, the receptionist and Ruth. Sensing he was about to bolt, Ruth removed the spray from her pocket and aimed it at his face.

"Call the police," she told the receptionist, jumping on Jake's back.

David Strong, the manager, emerged from his office. "What the hell is going on here?"

"Help me. Please, you have to help me restrain him," Ruth shouted, tussling with the bucking Jake. She grasped him tighter around his neck, determined not to let go.

"Get off me! Let go of me!" Jake sneered, trying desperately to release himself from her arms.

"No way. I will not let you get away."

Strong leapt over the reception desk and grabbed one of Jake's arms. Jake swung out with the other and struck the hotel manager on the nose.

Blood covered his face. "You broke it."

"Good. Get this woman off me." Jake staggered towards the main entrance.

"Help me. Don't let him get to the front door."

Sirens wailed in the distance. *Thank God, the cavalry's arriving. Hang on tight, girl.*

Out of the corner of her eye, she saw Strong pick up something. He raced towards them, the object held high. He yelled and smashed the vase over Jake's head. He toppled to the floor with Ruth. He was out cold. Strong helped Ruth to her feet. She brushed herself down and turned to see Inspector Littlejohn standing in the doorway.

"What's going on here?" Her gaze shot between Strong, Ruth, Fiona, and Jake lying prostrate on the floor.

Ruth pointed at Jake. "I've just caught your killer. Steven Swanson is an innocent man."

Littlejohn's mouth dropped open.

The receptionist cleared her throat with a slight cough. "I have his confession on my phone. I recorded it."

Ruth glanced her way and gave Maria a grateful smile.

Littlejohn stepped forward as her partner got on the phone for backup.

"I told you Steven didn't do it," Ruth insisted.

"You'll be required to come down to the station to make a state-ment," Littlejohn said. She moved closer to Ruth and slapped a hand on her shoulder. "Well done. Your tenacity worked out for you in the end."

Ruth was taken aback by the woman's unexpected praise. All she could think to say in response was, "Thank you."

EPILOGUE

*R*uth followed Littlejohn's car back to the station. She sat in the reception area for a few minutes until her impatience got the better of her, then she paced back and forth in front of the desk sergeant.

"For goodness' sake, Ruth, you're making me feel dizzy. Will you sit down?"

"Come on. How long does it take to release a wronged man?"

"The inspector will need to clear it with the Crown Prosecution Service first, you know that."

"What a load of poppycock! Come on, give the man a break. Can I at least see him? There's no harm in me doing that, is there? We all know he's innocent now. He's hardly a threat, not that he ever was in the first place. I tried to tell you all that, but no, you wouldn't listen to me."

The desk sergeant placed his hands over his ears. "La la la."

Despite the anger building up inside, Ruth giggled at the sergeant's antics. "All right. You win. I'll shut up, only if you let me in there to see him."

"Let me call the inspector, get the all clear from her." He picked up the phone and turned his back on her to speak to the inspector. When he finished his call, he grabbed a bunch of keys off a hook behind him and motioned for her to join him at the door. "The inspector says to give you ten minutes, if only to give us all a bit of peace and quiet."

"Yay, thank you. I knew I'd break you down eventually."

He tutted and led the way down the grimy grey corridor. When he opened the door, Steven immediately sat up on his bed.

"Ruth? What are you doing here?"

She inched past the sergeant's rotund stomach.

"Ten minutes," he reminded her before he slammed the door shut.

Ruth rushed to sit next to Steven and gathered his hands in hers.

"What are you doing here?" Steven repeated, confused.

She beamed at him. "I've caught the real killer. They're making the arrangements now to set you free. We did it, Steven!"

He withdrew his hands from her, covered his face and sobbed.

Ruth flung an arm around his shoulder and pulled him towards her. "There, there, you're going to be fine. This nightmare will be over soon, I promise you."

His hands dropped, and he clung to her. "It's been awful. How could they ever suspect I'd do such a thing?"

"I'm not making excuses for them, but they had to go with the evidence presented to them. You had her blood on your hands, love. It doesn't matter. You're going to be freed."

He pulled away and stared at her as if he still couldn't process the fact. "Who was it?"

"The daughter's boyfriend, Jake. He told me it was an accident. The jury will throw that out when it gets to court. You're free to get on with your life. That's the good news, Steven."

He let out a shuddering breath. "I don't think I'll ever get over this, Ruth. The community will treat me differently from now on, I just know they will."

"Not if I have anything to do with it. I'll make sure they all know this has been a huge mistake on the part of the police."

He shook his head. "Maybe we should leave things as they are. Accept that mistakes happen in this life and move on."

"We can do that. I'm delighted for you, Steven."

"None of this would have happened if it hadn't been for you fighting in my corner, Ruth. I'll be forever grateful to you for saving my life. I know if they had transferred me out of here today, I would have killed myself. I wouldn't have been able to cope."

"I think you're wrong. You're made of stronger stuff than that. Steven, I have to ask what you meant when I found you outside Jilly's room. You said 'not again'."

"It was back at university. My roommate committed suicide. I tried my hardest to resuscitate him, but it was too late. The only difference back then was the police officer in charge of the case believed me."

"How awful for you to go through all this a second time."

"I won't be so keen to help someone in the same predicament in the future, I can tell you."

Ruth turned when the key was inserted in the lock and the heavy door squeaked as it opened.

"Time's up, Ruth," the desk sergeant insisted.

Ruth held Steven's face in her hands and kissed him on the nose. "I'll be waiting for you."

He smiled. "You're an angel in disguise. Thank you, cherub."

Ruth walked out of the cell. At the end of the hallway stood James.

"Hello, you. I'm sorry for snapping at you."

He reached for her and gathered her in his arms. Against her neck, he whispered, "I was so worried about you."

"I was fine. I knew who the killer was. I just had to worm the information out of him."

"I'm sorry for ever doubting you."

Ruth slapped his arm and pushed away from him. "There's no need to apologise. One day you'll learn to accept I know what I'm talking about." She grinned and kissed him on the lips.

The desk sergeant walked past and groaned. "Get a room you two!"

They both laughed. The tension of the day seeped out of her. She puffed out her chest with pride at her achievements.

Against all the odds, she had managed to prove Steven's innocence. Life just didn't get better than this…

THE END

NOTE TO THE READER

Dear Reader,

What a heart-wrenching read that was.

But Ruth came to the rescue one of her dearest friends and proved DI Littlejohn wrong yet again.

Don't miss yet another daring adventure for Ruth to solve when another of her friends seeks her help after one of her visitors, a stranger to Carmel Cove goes missing.

Grab **Murder By The Sea**

Thank you for your support as always.

M A Comley

Reviews are a fantastic way of reaching out and showing an author how much you appreciate their work – so leave one today, if you will.

Made in the USA
Middletown, DE
11 December 2019